*Frank's homecoming crushed Amy's spirit and filled her with fear.*

Amy pushed her chair back and hurried across the room. She knew the family was watching, that they would hear every word, but she was beyond caring. She wanted to fling her arms around Frank and hold him until he could feel her love passing between them.

Instead she reached for his hand. He shrank back a bit from her touch but not completely. Was he afraid to show rudeness to her in front of his family? she wondered. She folded her hands around his hand and spoke quietly. "I'm glad you're home. I hate the things you've endured, but I'm so glad you're alive and back with us. I love you."

Time seemed to stretch forever while she waited for him to respond. His gaze searched hers somewhat warily. She thought he grew more tired before her eyes. "I'm all in, Amy. Can we talk another time?"

"Of course."

He tugged his hand lightly, and she released it.

Jason came across the kitchen with a newly lit kerosene lamp, and he and Frank headed upstairs.

The ache in Amy's chest grew to enormous proportions. *He didn't say he loves me, not once.*

**JOANN A. GROTE** lives in Minnesota, where she grew up. She uses the state for most of her story settings, and like her characters, JoAnn seeks to serve Christ in her work. She believes that readers of novels can receive a message of salvation and encouragement from well-crafted fiction. She has had several novels published with Barbour Publishing in the **Heartsong Presents** line as well as in the **American Adventure** series for kids.

Books by JoAnn A. Grote

**HEARTSONG PRESENTS**

HP36—The Sure Promise
HP51—The Unfolding Heart
HP55—Treasure of the Heart
HP103—Love's Shining Hope
HP120—An Honest Love
HP136—Rekindled Flame
HP184—Hope That Sings
HP288—Sweet Surrender
HP331—A Man for Libby
HP377—Come Home to My Heart
HP476—Hold on My Heart

# Meet Me with a Promise

*JoAnn A. Grote*

Heartsong Presents

*For Charlie*

**A note from the author:**
*I love to hear from my readers! You may correspond with me by writing:*

**JoAnn A. Grote**
**Author Relations**
**PO Box 719**
**Uhrichsville, OH 44683**

**ISBN 1-58660-610-7**

**MEET ME WITH A PROMISE**





*Cover design by Lorraine Bush.*

PRINTED IN THE U.S.A.

# one

*Chippewa City, Minnesota*
*April 27, 1898*

Frank Sterling knocked on the oak door at the top of the narrow indoor stairway and waited. He'd traveled 130 miles, from St. Paul to Chippewa City on the edge of the prairie, to see Amy. He shifted his wide-brimmed brown hat from his right hand to his left and shifted his weight impatiently from one foot to the other.

From the street below he'd seen the mellow glow of lamplight filter through the lace curtains in the window of the second-story apartment Amy Henderson and her father shared above Dr. Matt Strong's pharmacy. One of them must be home.

Were those footsteps? He stopped fidgeting and straightened. The brass doorknob turned, and the door opened. His heart quickened at the sight of Amy in a simple white shirtwaist and dark blue skirt, her pale brown hair in the popular upsweep, as usual. "Hello, Amy."

The green-gold eyes he loved widened. Joy filled her face and reflected in his heart. "Frank."

She threw her arms about his neck, and he caught her to himself. The familiar lavender fragrance filled his senses.

The uncharacteristic spontaneity of her greeting warmed him. He realized suddenly what was meant by the saying "Home is where the heart is." This was his home, no matter where he lived. Home was with Amy, in her arms, in each other's hearts.

"The war's come, Amy." His voice broke slightly on the

words. He hugged his fiancée close, trying to surround her with enough love to protect them both from what the future might hold.

"I know." Her hug tightened a moment before she released her hold. She stood in the circle of his arms and played with the collar of his brown corduroy jacket. "Word arrived in town over the wire at the railroad station yesterday. Men galloped through the streets, shouting the news like Paul Revere calling out the minutemen. I'm afraid the editor of the *Chippewa City Commercial* is a bit miffed he wasn't the one to break the story to the town."

Frank managed a lame laugh at her joke. He knew from her high, bright tone that she was trying to be cheerful and brave for him. He'd play along.

She gave his collar a final pat and stepped back, breaking the circle of his arms. "My, what am I thinking, keeping you out here on the landing? Come in."

He followed her into the living area, reaching quickly to grasp one of her hands. She darted a surprised smile at him over her shoulder. He squeezed her hand and returned the smile.

His gaze swept the small room. Fine furniture from the large home the Hendersons once owned crowded the room: mahogany tables, pale blue satin parlor chairs and matching brocade sofa, and the grandfather clock that once stood in their hallway. There was no hallway for the clock here. A fine gateleg table was tucked in one corner, covered with lace and bordered by two chairs with needlepoint cushions. The corner was the Hendersons' current dining area. There was no dining room in the tiny apartment. In the opposite corner stood Mr. Henderson's imposing mahogany desk.

Pale blue velvet draperies hung beside exquisite lace under-curtains, further remnants from the home on the hill, the home that had been the envy of the town. Porcelain figurines rested on tables and graced shelves. Books from her father's once pretentious library filled the walls and were piled here and there on the thick Persian carpet. The lamp on the piecrust table before one of the two windows in the room sent light through the pink roses on the painted globe.

The panic of 1893 had wiped out Mr. Henderson's investments and taken the house, but he and Amy never complained about their cramped new home. Frank admired their attitude. It had made him love Amy more than he had before her father's financial disaster.

The silence of the apartment registered on him. "Isn't your father home?"

"He's meeting with Dr. Strong about some missionary board business before tonight's prayer meeting."

Frank took a step toward the door. "I shouldn't stay." He didn't want to hurt her reputation. All it would take in this small town was one person discovering they were here alone and Amy would be top gossip news for days.

A rosy blush tinted Amy's cheeks. "I was so excited to see you that I forgot Father isn't here to act as chaperon. Would you like to go to the prayer meeting? It's a special one because of the war. It begins in about twenty minutes."

"I can't think of a more appropriate place to be right now than at a prayer meeting with our friends." He glanced at the parlor stove's grate to see if a fire needed to be banked before they left. No light shown through. The late April evenings were still cool, but the Hendersons had chosen not to heat the apartment. He opened the door and stood just outside on the landing to wait for her.

Amy slipped on a blue jacket that matched her skirt. The jacket nipped in at the waist. It's wide lapels and popular leg-o'-mutton sleeves increased the impression of a willowy frame. After adding a matching hat and gloves, she put out the lamp, and she and Frank left.

Frank liked the familiar feel of Amy's fingers tucked into the crook of his arm, her shoulder brushing gently against his as they walked, the soft sound of her skirt swishing as her shoes kept up a light *tap-tap* beside his heavier tread on the boardwalk. The realization their time together was limited caused an ache in his throat and chest.

He tipped his hat to the lamplighter who was busy lighting the lamps along Main Street against the darkening twilight. Most shops had closed for the day, and there weren't many people walking or riding along the street.

Flags waved from every storefront. Red, white, and blue bunting draped from balconies and the tops of buildings. It hadn't taken the nation long to break out in a nationalistic fervor.

"Flags are everywhere in St. Paul, too," Frank told Amy. "On the trip out here, flags and bunting flew from every station and from farmhouses, too. Even saw a milk farmer with a flag perched on his wagon. Stores have about run out of flags."

"Here, too."

They started up the steps leading to the top of the ridge. Most businesses were built along Main Street near the river at the bottom of the ridge. The homes and churches perched on the prairie above.

"I didn't expect to see you, Frank. It's Wednesday. Didn't you have classes?" She stopped suddenly and stared up at him with questioning eyes. "Surely the university didn't close because of the war?"

He gave a short laugh. "Hardly. I came home to see you." He pressed her arm closer to his side. "You know I joined the National Guard a few weeks ago."

"Yes, after the *Maine* was fired upon."

"I joined because I believe we as a nation should be prepared to fight for others who are struggling for their freedom. Maybe I was naive, but I believed if Spain knew we were serious about helping the Cubans gain their freedom, Spain would withdraw from Cuba. We now know Spain is ready to fight us to stay there."

"Yes, unfortunately for everyone."

"I don't want to kill anyone, Amy. I don't even like killing the hogs and chickens we raise on the farm. And I'm not sure if Spain meant the *Maine* to hit the mines in Havana Harbor. Like everyone else, I hate that we lost the 266 men who were aboard on a peace mission, but my conscience won't let me stand by and do nothing when we can help the Cuban people. The stories we hear about the way they've been treated by the Spanish—" He couldn't think of words to tell how the horror affected him.

Amy squeezed his arm. "I know. It's impossible to imagine people treat others the way the news stories say the Cubans are treated. Herded into guarded camps surrounded by barbed wire and hunted down like animals. I read that almost two hundred thousand Cubans have been killed."

Frank nodded. "Yes, almost a quarter of their people."

They walked along the boardwalk that edged the top of the ridge. Across the road, houses looked out over the river valley. Children darted among the houses, hiding behind bushes and trees. "Ally, ally, ally in free!" they heard a girl call.

Amy smiled up at him. "Remember playing that when you were a child?"

"Yes, but I played with my brothers and sisters on the farm, not with my neighbors, like you must have done being an only child."

"It was fun just the same. How was your trip out today?"

"Fine. Long. The train seemed crowded for a weekday. Everyone was talking about the war, of course."

Two boys darted across the street. Frank and Amy stopped as the boys ran past and down the slope. One carried a wooden rifle. The other a wooden sword. "Remember the

*Maine!"* the second boy cried.

Amy shivered and drew closer to Frank. He laid his hand over her fingers where they rested on his arm. "It's only play," he said quietly.

She nodded and smiled brightly. "I just had a chill. I should have expected it would turn colder now that the sun's down. Spring afternoons feel so warm after the long, cold winter."

Her bravado didn't fool him, but he didn't challenge it. He was glad for her courage. It was easier to face than the fear she must feel at the thought of the war. It was easier to face than his own fears.

The simple event silenced the announcement he'd traveled almost all the way across Minnesota to make to her. The words filled him and pushed to be told, but the dread of seeing her eyes darken in sadness and fear kept the words inside. He suspected she knew what he'd come to say, but as long as the words were unspoken, they could pretend there was escape from the truth.

More people and carriages filled the walks and streets as they passed the tall brick high school and neared the church. He was pleased to see his brother Jason's horses and wagon hitched outside. He'd be able to ride back to the farm with Jason for the night. Besides, Jason and the rest of the family had to be told, too.

People greeted Frank and Amy with surprised, happy faces as the couple neared the church. There wasn't time for long hellos since the church bells were announcing the prayer meeting was about to begin. Frank knew that wouldn't be the case following the service. Neighbors and family would want to know what he was doing home in the middle of the week. It wasn't his nature to lie to them.

It wouldn't be right not to tell Amy before she overheard him telling others. He drew her aside just outside the tall, heavy wooden doors. "I have to tell you. I should have told you earlier, I know, but. . ."

The soft lines of her sweet young face drooped. Her eyes lost a bit of their light, as if to ward off a blow, but her gaze met his unflinching.

He took a deep breath before continuing in a whisper. "The first troops for the war are to be called from the National Guard. I expect the call to come any day now. That's why I came home, to say good-bye."

❧

Amy sat between her father and Frank on the hard wooden pew. She followed the words of the prayers issued by Reverend Conrad and others, her heart pleading their essence as never before. Prayers for a quick war, for few casualties, for victory and freedom for the Cuban people rumbled out in Reverend Conrad's deep, comforting voice.

*Let Spain change its mind, even at this late hour, Lord,* Amy's own heart pleaded. *Let war be averted and the Cuban people win their freedom without further bloodshed. If this can't be, please bring Frank home safe to me.*

The prayer rang over and over inside her head. Frank had to come home. He had to. All her plans were wrapped up in him. How would she be able to go on if he didn't return?

Tears heated her eyes. She batted them back. She wouldn't let herself cry. She wouldn't burden Frank with her own fears. He needed to know she supported him in his decision.

Frank's family filled the pew in front of them: his older brother, Jason; Jason's wife, Pearl; their three-year-old son, Chalmers, and three-month-old daughter, Viola; seventeen-year-old Andy; sixteen-year-old Maggie; and ten-year-old Grace. With their brown hair and wide faces, none of them looked anything like Frank. Amy loved his almost black hair and matching thin mustache, the somber dark eyes that were as black as his hair when he was angry, the square jaw, and quiet, reserved manner.

Frank's parents were no longer with them; they'd been killed in an accident five years earlier. Grace and Chalmers kept turning to peek over the top of the pew at Frank with big grins. Normally their antics amused Amy. Tonight their actions were bittersweet.

Frank squeezed her hand. Her eyes misted over once more. She didn't look at him but kept her gaze on her lap. Frank had been right. This was the best place to be, surrounded by their friends and family, seeking God's comfort and help. It was absolutely the perfect place to be.

After the service, Frank's family surrounded him with hugs and the question Amy knew they'd ask. Friends broke through the family circle to ask the same question. "What are you doing home in the middle of the week? Did the university kick you out?" followed by friendly laughter.

Amy kept a smile on her face through all the answers, through the repeat of the same answer so many times she lost count. She hated the answer.

"You must be so proud of him," people said to her over and over.

She nodded and said, "Yes, I am."

It was true. She was proud of him. Proud of his beautiful heart that cried out against one group of people trying to overpower another. Proud that he was the kind of man who was more than talk, the kind of man who stood up for what he said he believed.

And completely terrified he might not come home alive.

The town's young men formed a tight circle around Frank, soon forcing most of his family aside.

"Wish I'd thought to join up with the guard," Roland, a redheaded young man who'd attended the local academy with Frank, blustered. "Maybe I'll volunteer for the navy instead, though."

"Me, too," Frank's brother Andy agreed. "We might need

the army to get the Spanish soldiers off the island, but I'd sure like to have a shot at their ships. After all, they blew up the *Maine*. That's what started all this."

Pearl, who was standing behind Amy, gasped. Beside her, Jason groaned.

Amy studied Andy uneasily. He wasn't that much younger than she and Frank, but Andy seemed barely out of boyhood.

The smile on Frank's face died. "Are you serious, Andy?"

"'Course I'm serious."

Jason shook his head. "We need you on the farm, Andy."

Andy pushed back a hunk of his straight brown hair and jutted out his chin. "The country needs me, too. I'm almost eighteen. I won't need your permission to sign up."

The group about them fell silent. Jason and Andy glared at each other. Feet shifted as the group watched the brothers.

Frank slipped an arm around Andy's shoulders. "Let's talk about your plans at home tonight."

Andy grinned at him. "Sure."

The conversation started up again slowly with Roland asking Frank how he'd come to join the guard.

Amy watched Andy, disquiet filling her spirit. Andy and Frank had squabbled for years, as so many brothers did. Suddenly Andy was acting like Frank was a hero because he was likely to be in a war soon. Would Frank try to talk Andy out of following him into the service, or would he encourage Andy to join up? It would be difficult enough for their family to have one of the brothers in danger. Amy hoped Andy could be persuaded to stay home. She grudgingly acknowledged to herself that the farm couldn't possibly sound as exciting to a boy Andy's age as fighting in a war.

Her gaze traveled around the ring of young men and boys. Their eyes were lit with unsuppressed excitement. Their voices were loud with it. All of them were eager to be part of avenging the Cuban people and shoving the Spanish out of the Western Hemisphere. They reminded her of the two boys who'd run across her and Frank's path earlier, playing at war.

Reverend Conrad broke through the circle of young men. His bearded, lean face and deep-set eyes were sober as he rested one of his hands on Frank's shoulder. "I hear you're likely to be called up soon."

"Yes, Sir." Pride and excitement shone in Frank's eyes.

"I wish we'd known sooner. We could have prayed for you tonight during the meeting. You can be sure we'll be praying for you from here on."

"Thank you, Sir. That means a lot to me."

Amy smiled her own thanks to the preacher. The promised prayers gave comfort, reminding her that whatever happened, she and Frank were wrapped in the love of the Lord and their friends.

"So you're going to be a soldier." A round man, so short he barely reached Frank's shoulder, slapped Frank on the back.

It apparently took Frank, who was engrossed in conversation with Jason, by surprise. He stumbled forward a step, coughing. Turning, he recognized his friendly attacker and grinned. "Hi, Shorty. Yes, I'm with the guard."

Shorty hitched at his trousers. "Nothing like fighting for your country, no siree." His lips twisted into a proud, tight smile.

A tall, lean, wrinkled man beside Shorty snorted. "A lot you know about it. You didn't fight for your country. You fought against it, you low-down Confederate."

Shorty's ruddy complexion grew redder. "Did so fight for my country, Slim Anders. We'd withdrawn from the Union, as was our right. We were dragged back into it kicking and screaming."

Slim rested both hands on the top of his cane and leaned over Shorty. "And you're still screaming about it. Think you'd have enough sense to thank us Yanks for letting you stay part of the greatest country on the face of the earth."

Shorty's eyes narrowed. *"Letting* us *stay?"* He reached up and pointed one of his index fingers at the bottom of Slim's nose. "We had a pretty good country of our own. That's why the Union didn't want us to go. We're the part that makes this the greatest country on the face of the earth."

The group around them chuckled. Amy smiled. They'd all heard the same arguments and more every time the two men were within speaking distance of each other. They'd been arguing since they arrived in Chippewa City almost thirty years ago.

Frank raised his hands, palms out. "Truce. This is a house of peace, remember?"

"Hmmmph." Shorty crossed his arms over his chest. "At least in this war the North and South will be fighting together against the same enemy."

Slim nodded curtly. "You finally got something right." He patted Frank's shoulder. "You do us proud in this war, young Sterling, you hear?"

Frank grinned. "Yes, Sir. I'll do my best."

Amy noticed Reverend Conrad had begun putting out the lamps. She touched Frank's arm and nodded in the direction of the preacher. "I think it's time to leave."

They and the group around them filed down the aisle toward the door. They walked slowly, letting Slim set the pace. He was so tall and sure of himself that Amy tended to forget he had a wooden leg. As far as she could tell, it only slowed down his walking. The man was spry of mind and as energetic as a man half his age. In spite of the way he and Shorty bickered, both men were loved by the community. She couldn't imagine the town without them.

Once outside, Jason turned to Frank. "Pearl and I are heading over to Pearl's parents with the young'ns to visit. You can meet up with us there later and ride back to the farm, if you'd like."

"Thanks, I'll do that."

Jason jerked his thumb toward the line of wagons and horses hitched along the street. "There's an extra lantern in the wagon box if you need one."

"Good. Amy and I didn't think to bring one along, and her father already left with Dr. Strong."

Townspeople who lived along the way kept Frank and Amy company as they walked, exchanging pleasantries. A group of older boys followed behind, singing "Rally 'Round the Flag, Boys." The words sent icy shivers down Amy's spine.

She was glad when the last of the boys and their families turned to their homes, leaving her and Frank alone. The lantern of blackened tin swung from one of Frank's hands, making shadows on the boardwalk.

Amy and Frank started down the wooden stairs that ran from the top of the ridge to Main Street. Once they reached the street, there would be no privacy. The stairway to the apartment was private, but her father would arrive home soon. She desperately wanted a little more time alone with Frank. "Do you think we could stop here for a few minutes and talk?"

"Here?"

She heard the surprise and hesitance in his voice. The ridge was covered with brush, making the steps a secluded area. She knew it had a reputation as an area for spooning couples in the warmer months. Her cheeks heated, and she was glad Frank couldn't see them color in the dark. "I only want to talk with you alone." She sat down on the cold wood.

Frank sat down beside her and set the lantern a couple steps below them. "We shouldn't bump it there." He slipped an arm around her and pulled her close. "Ah, Amy, I'm going to miss you awfully."

She rested her cheek on his shoulder. "I'll miss you, too." It felt so comfortably familiar, being with him like this. She loved the way it felt to be in his arms. "What will happen with your education, Frank? Will the university allow you to graduate without completing this year's studies?"

"I'll go back when the war's over. Everyone says it won't last long."

No one had thought the War Between the States would last long, either, if she remembered her history lessons correctly.

"My graduation will just have to be postponed." He cleared his throat. The sound was loud in the night, so close to her ear. "I'm afraid the wedding we planned for June will have to be postponed, too. I'm so sorry, Amy."

She nodded against his shoulder, his corduroy jacket soft beneath her cheek. Her throat was thick with unshed tears. She couldn't speak, but it didn't matter since there were no words that could change things. War was one of the unfightable things in life. Leaders decided to wage war, and the lives and plans of their countrymen went up in smoke.

Amy felt Frank's lips warm against her temple. She didn't dare lift her lips for his kiss, afraid she wouldn't be able to hold back the tears.

"I know it seems unfair," he whispered. "We've waited so long to be together. There're so many things we fought to have the right to be man and wife. I'll never forget how close I came to losing you to Walter Bay."

Amy shuddered. "Don't remind me." Walter had tried to coerce her into marrying him to save her father's house, on which Walter held the mortgage. Amy had thought she was being noble, agreeing to marry the man to save her father's home. Thanks to Frank, she'd finally realized her father wouldn't want her to sacrifice herself that way. Walter now resided in prison. "I had a narrow escape."

"*We* had a narrow escape, my love. We've had a lot of escapes. If it weren't for your father refusing to allow me to see you unless I quit drinking, no telling what my life would be like now." He pulled his head back, and she glanced up at him. "I expect you wouldn't have stuck by me if I'd kept up the drinking and gambling."

She smiled. The lantern didn't cast enough light to see his features, which were further shadowed by his hat brim. "I suppose you're right, but it's so hard for me to believe you ever did those things. I never saw you drunk."

"For which I'm eternally grateful."

This time she had no qualms in meeting his kiss. It was warm and gentle and sweet and filled with his love, as she remembered. How long after tonight until they shared a kiss again?

A sliver of an idea slipped into her mind. She blinked in surprise. Blinked again. The idea put out a root into her heart. It wasn't all that far-fetched, was it?

She fingered one of the bone buttons on Frank's jacket. "Frank, about the wedding. . ."

"Yes?"

"We wouldn't have to postpone it. We could cancel it instead."

She felt him stiffen. It seemed even his breathing stopped for a moment. "Cancel it?"

"Well, not exactly cancel it. What's the opposite of postpone?"

He pulled back slightly. "What are you talking about?"

"The wedding."

"I know, but—"

"Do we have to get married when you get back from the war?"

"I thought you wanted to get married." His voice was defensive, threaded with confusion. "I thought you loved me. That's why we planned the wedding, isn't it? Isn't that what we've wanted for years?"

She laughed softly, joyous in the knowledge of his love for her. "Yes, that's what we want. So why wait? Why not get married right away, before you leave?"

# two

"Marry now? Tonight?" Frank jerked back and grabbed Amy's shoulders, a jolt of energy rushing through him.

"Yes, or as soon as possible." He felt her breath soft against his face with her quiet laugh. "Why not?"

"Why not? There are a million reasons why not."

She slid her arms around his waist. Her lips touched his cheek in a quick, warm kiss. "No, there's not. We love each other, and we want to be married. There are not a million reasons we shouldn't be married right away. There's not one reason we shouldn't."

"There's at least one very good reason, and you know it. You just don't want to admit it." He grasped her shoulders again and pushed her gently from him. Her suggestion was all too tempting when she was so close. He stood up to further break the intangible bond.

She rose quickly, all but destroying his attempt at defense. The lavender scent she wore melded once again with the spring earth smells. "What is that reason?"

"Are you sure that's what you want, for me to put it into words?"

Even in the darkness he could see the outline of her face, see her chin lift. "Yes. Say it."

"I could die, Amy. I might not come back." The anger in his voice shocked him. "I could die," he repeated, forcing a softness he didn't feel to the words.

"Why should that keep us from marrying?" she challenged. "I'd be as alone then whether we married or not."

He was sure she knew he would like to be married as much

as she wanted it. "You haven't thought this through."

"To what conclusion?"

"If we married, we might have a child."

"Yes."

The love and happiness in the word almost crushed his resolve. "That can't happen, Amy."

"Why not? You love children."

"It's irresponsible to father a child when a man knows he might not be there to raise it."

"No man knows he'll be there to raise his children. It doesn't take war to kill a man. Your sister Grace was only five when your parents died. Besides, not all soldiers die when they go to war—not even most of them."

Frank groaned and wrapped his arms around her. "You are too convincing for our own good."

She leaned against his chest, her shoulders shaking in soft laughter. "Does that mean you agree to my proposal?"

"I'd love to, but I can't." He sighed. "You know I'm right about this, Amy."

She wasn't laughing any longer. "You'll come back, Frank. You must." She paused, and he suspected it was to swallow the desperation he heard in her words. "But on the slight chance you don't, if we marry, you might have a child keeping part of you alive."

He understood now what she wanted—a way to keep him and their dreams and their love alive if he didn't make it back. "It wouldn't be fair to the child," he whispered. "We mustn't pretend that it would be."

He pulled her closer and rocked slightly, wishing he could comfort them both. He wanted to tell her it would be all right, he'd be back, but he had a bad feeling about this war. Not about his decision to fight in it—the Cuban people's freedom from Spanish tyranny was worth risking his life.

"When I return, we'll have so many babies, we'll need two

houses to hold our family."

"Enough babies to fill our arms and hearts will be fine." Tears mingled with her words.

Frank wasn't sure how long they stood that way, holding each other, speaking only with their hearts. Finally he picked up the lantern, and he and Amy walked to her home. His chest felt as though it would explode with his love for her and with the fear they wouldn't have the life together they'd dreamed of for so long and the fear that their babies would only live in their dreams.

❧

Frank leaned back against the side of the wooden wagon box with his younger siblings. Old quilts and fragrant, scratchy straw lessened the jolts slightly as the family headed down the rutted country road under the stars toward home.

Jason's son, Chalmers, slept in Frank's lap, oblivious to the bouncing. Frank studied the round face resting trustingly against his chest. Chalmers's expression beneath pale brown curls was calm in the moonlight. Remembering his discussion with Amy only an hour earlier, Frank's chest expanded in gratitude for this cherished time. Would he ever cradle his and Amy's son in his arms?

He glanced across the wagon bed at Andy. The boy's head rolled easily back and forth with the wagon's movements. His eyes were closed, and his arms crossed over his chest. Frank was pretty sure his brother wasn't sleeping but rather choosing to ignore the rest of the family's friendly chatter to show his anger at Jason. Frank felt sorry for him, walling himself off that way, but maybe his sullen ways were better than subjecting everyone else to his rage.

When they arrived at the farm, Andy took the still-sleeping Chalmers from Frank and started toward the house. Pearl followed with baby Viola. Maggie ran ahead to open the back door off the porch and light a lamp.

Frank reached to help his youngest sister, Grace, out of the wagon bed. The ten year old hugged him tightly about the neck, refusing to be lowered to the ground. Her giggle tickled his ear, and he laughed with her.

"Better get down, Pumpkin," he warned, "or you'll have to help me rub down the horses."

"I don't mind." Her hold didn't slacken a whit.

"On second thought, you're too short to help with the horses. You barely reach their bellies."

"I'm not either that short."

"I'll have to set you down to work on the horses. What if you fall asleep in the barn?"

Her giggle rose. "You'd carry me into the house."

"I might forget you."

"No, you wouldn't."

She was right, of course. "Jason, I'll be out to help unhitch after I take Grace inside."

Grace's game continued in the kitchen, where Maggie had lit the kerosene lamp on the red-and-white oilcloth-covered table. It took the promise that the youngster could help him milk the cows in the morning to convince her to release her hold.

"Can I shoot milk to the cats right from the cows?" she pleaded.

He ruffled her hair. "We'll see how good your aim is."

Frank smiled as he hurried across the farmyard in the moonlight to the large red barn, his shoes kicking up dust. He would have been impatient with his youngest sister for such a performance in the past. Knowing he might be called to battle changed his attitude toward even such previously insignificant exchanges.

Smells of animals and of fields freshly plowed for spring seeding and of leaves budding out drifted on the night air. The windmill creaked as it turned in the prairie breeze. A wolf howled somewhere out in the night. Stars blinked, and the moon hung in a sky that seemed to go on forever. Frank drank the night in with all his senses and wondered what night was like in Cuba.

Jason was finishing unhitching, while the horses stamped impatiently outside the barn door. The horses needed no urging to enter the barn, where rest and water and food waited. They went right to adjoining stalls. The saddle horses in nearby stalls whinnied a greeting.

Andy brought buckets of water for rubbing down the horses. Together the three brothers made sure the horses had fresh water, hay, and corn.

Frank performed the chores, all the time aware of enjoying the feel of the barn at night: the creak of the building; the strong, warm smell of the horses; the cats watching patiently, then darting into the straw in the hope of catching any little creature foolish enough to stir; the larger animals moving about and crunching straw beneath their hooves.

When the duties toward the horses were completed for the evening, Frank patted each of the horses' necks. "Be sure you're good to these guys while I'm gone," he admonished his brothers.

"I'll take good care of them," Andy promised. The brothers started for the door. Andy reached for the lantern and shot Frank a grin. "At least until I enlist."

*He can't wait to leave the farm and ordinary, everyday life, and I can't wait to get back to the farm and ordinary, everyday life. Maybe there'll be a miracle, and the Cubans will be allowed their freedom, the Spaniards will go home, and Andy and I and Amy can stay home and live plain, dull, ordinary lives.*

*Please, God.*

❧

Frank rode one of the saddle horses to town the next morning after helping Jason and Andy milk the cows. He smiled, remembering Grace's play with the cows and cats. Her attempts at milking were short-lived.

He'd taken a few minutes to say good-bye to his favorite cows, especially Sudsy, and Gideon, the one-eyed golden tabby cat who'd been a good friend since a kitten. He was going to miss those animals. He already missed them while attending the university, but that was different.

Even the fields he passed triggered unfamiliar emotions within him. For the first spring of his life he wouldn't be here when the fields turned green with new crops. He wouldn't see the crops grow tall and lush, see them waving in the summer breezes, hear the wind clatter through them, or watch the sunlight and shadows play over them. Would he be back in time for harvest? Those people most optimistic about the United States' power might consider it possible, but he doubted it, even if the war was short.

On reaching town, he made only one stop before heading to Amy's. He tried to keep his desire to be alone with Amy at bay during a meal of scalloped oysters with Amy and her father. As soon as Frank felt he could politely do so, he suggested that he and Amy go for a walk.

The couple didn't speak of where to walk but, as if in unspoken agreement, headed behind Main Street toward the river that wound through the valley beneath sheltering cottonwoods.

Some of the cottonwoods stood in water, for winter's melting snows made the river high. It rushed over its banks in a muddy, dangerous wash along its usual path and beyond. The flooding wasn't high enough to threaten the businesses on Main Street this year, but farmers' fields on the other side of the river lay beneath swirling water.

Frank selected a spot beneath a cottonwood not far from the edge of the water. He removed something from his jacket pocket and spread his corduroy jacket on the ground. "Sit here, Amy."

"That isn't necessary. I don't want to get your jacket dirty."

"Better my jacket than your skirt. Besides, the air is warm, but the ground still holds a bit of winter's chill. I wouldn't want you to get cold."

"I should have thought to bring a quilt."

*Nothing talk,* Frank thought. Nothing but unimportant details to hide the fact that inside they both felt like the careening waters before them, out of control and running over life's familiar edges.

Seated beside her, he reached for one of her hands and wished she weren't wearing the blue cotton gloves that matched the blue background in her dress. He couldn't recall ever seeing her outside without her hat and gloves. He was accustomed to Pearl and his sisters often going without both outside at the farm.

Frank touched the brim of her hat with his index finger. "I don't think I've seen your hair uncovered in the sunshine since before we entered high school."

Her cheeks flushed and her lashes lowered. "It wouldn't be proper." She shifted slightly until her shoulder rested partly against his shoulder and partly against his chest. He sighed in contentment at her closeness.

He held out the maroon velvet box he'd removed from his jacket pocket. "This is for you."

Her eyes widened in surprise. She opened the box and gasped at the sight of the tiny ruby heart set on a silver ring. "Oh, Frank, it's beautiful."

He tenderly removed her glove, then slipped the ring on her finger. Her hand trembled slightly. He touched his lips to the ring and then lifted his gaze to hers. "I wanted you to have something, something you could keep with you all the time to remind you that I love you. I'll always love you. I'll go on loving you even if time stops."

Tears brightened her eyes. Then she was in his arms, her

arms around his neck. "I love you, Frank." Her tears tumbled over and flavored their kisses.

The thought that they should perhaps not be so intimate within sight of the backs of some Main Street buildings gave him only momentary pause. He held her close, feeling her heart beat strong and quick against his chest.

After a few minutes, she pulled back slightly in his arms. Her hat, pinned so primly in place with a pearl-studded pin before they left the apartment, hung askew over her left ear. She laughed self-consciously and removed the hat, setting it on the grass beside them. Her hair tumbled in loose waves from its topknot.

"I have something for you, too." She fumbled in her lace reticule and pulled out the folded brown paper he'd seen her slip into her apron pocket earlier. She handed it to him, her eyes shining above flushed cheeks.

He removed the red twine tied about the small package. It was fun to receive something unexpected from her. It didn't matter what the package held. "Feels solid," he remarked.

She only smiled, her eyes bright with expectation and the joy of giving. He leaned forward and kissed her lightly on the lips.

She pushed at his chest gently with her fingertips. "Open it."

He grinned at her eagerness and obeyed. A silver pocket watch embossed with a simple vine design lay in his hand. It wasn't expensive, but it must have cost her dearly. She and her father hadn't money to spend on extravagances.

"I want you to have something with you always to remind you of my love." Her voice was just above a whisper, almost drowned out by the splashing of the water rushing past. "My love, too, will live past time."

The words grew in meaning, connected as they were to the little time remaining before he left. He clutched the watch in his hand, unable to speak for the lump in his throat.

Amy unclasped his fingers from the watch. "Open it."

He pulled his gaze from her face and opened the watchcase. Opposite the watch face was a picture of Amy.

He slid his hand behind her neck and pulled her toward him. Their lips met in a sweet, lingering kiss. "The gift is perfect. You couldn't have given me anything I'd treasure more. I'll keep it with me always."

Her eyes told him that he and his heart had said just the right thing.

Amy cleared her throat and pointed to the still-open watchcase. "That is telling me it's time we started back. I have an art class at the academy this afternoon. It's the only class I teach today."

Regret that their time alone was ending washed through him, but he snapped the watch shut and stood.

Amy pushed at her loosened locks of hair, rearranging hairpins until the topknot again felt secure, then pinning on her little blue hat. She pulled her glove on over the ruby ring, and they reluctantly stood up, Frank putting on his jacket.

The couple walked slowly, her hand in the crook of his arm, shoulders brushing, treasuring these last few minutes together and the simple touches that seemed so intimate.

Mr. Henderson was just coming down the stairs of the second-floor apartment when Frank and Amy reached the first-floor pharmacy. They had barely exchanged greetings when they were interrupted. Feet sounded in a running, thumping pace on the boardwalk behind them. "Sterling! Frank Sterling, wait up!"

The three turned toward the voice. Frank's friend Roland was running toward them from the direction of the train station, his open jacket flapping and his red hair windswept. His right hand held a yellow paper, which he waved over his head as he ran.

Roland stopped beside them. "Glad I caught you." He

gasped for breath between sentences. "I was headed for the livery. Planned to ride out to your farm to let you know." He waved the rectangular piece of paper in Frank's direction.

Frank took it. He read it silently and felt the blood drain from his face. The stiffening went out of his knees. He lowered himself to the wooden bench in front of the pharmacy.

"What is it?" Amy grabbed the paper from him, fear drawing her eyebrows together in a frown. Her father peered over her shoulder.

Roland didn't wait for them to read the news. "The state guard's been called up. They're ordered to assemble in St. Paul tomorrow at Camp Ramsey with a day's cooked rations."

*It's too soon,* Frank thought. *Too soon.*

He'd known it was coming, but in spite of all his talk of it the last couple days, he felt numb all the way through. *It's too soon.*

# three

*It's too soon,* Amy thought. *I'm not ready for him to leave yet, Lord.*

She rested one of her hands on her chest. She could feel her heart beating as steady as always. How could that be, when she felt numb from head to toe?

Amy felt a hand on her shoulder and turned to see her father's sorrow-filled gaze upon her. "Maybe you could put together some food for him to eat on the train back."

She nodded.

Frank stood up. He removed his hat with one hand and pushed the fingers of his other hand through his hair. "That would be nice, thank you. Roland, would you mind riding out to the farm and letting my family know?"

"Sure. Already told the others at the station that I was heading out there. They won't be expecting me back for awhile."

"You can take my horse. I left it at the livery when I rode in this morning. Is it too late to catch a train back to St. Paul?"

"Leaves in an hour."

"Not much time." Frank settled his hat back on his head.

Roland was breathing easier now. He pulled his shoulders back and lifted his chin in a manner that made Amy think he was feeling important as the bearer of this awful news. He held out his hand. "In case I don't see you before you leave, good luck, old man. Give those Spaniards what for."

As Roland left, Amy turned toward the door to the apartment with a heavy heart. Frank and her father followed.

She was grateful her father went to his desk when they

entered the apartment, again leaving her and Frank alone in the kitchen.

Frank leaned against the cupboard while Amy sliced and buttered bread and put it in a tin lunch bucket for him. Her chest ached from unspoken words, but she didn't know what the words were, only the feeling of them.

"Can you spare any of that great pie you made this morning?" There was a forced lilt to Frank's voice.

Amy kept her back to him and managed to put a touch of lightness in her own voice. "I think I could spare a piece or two." Her jaw quivered. She clamped her lips shut. *I won't break down. I won't make this harder for him.*

She sliced the pie. As she put the pieces in the tin pail, she heard her father clear his throat loudly just before entering the kitchen. "You two youngsters ready to head to the train station yet?"

Frank straightened and picked up the tin pail by its handle. "Yes, Sir. Amy has packed me a fine lunch. I'm afraid I've taken the last of your pie, though."

Mr. Henderson patted his sizable stomach. "Oh, I think I'll make it through until the next pie is baked. It's near time for Amy's class."

Amy gasped and pressed her palms to her cheeks. "I forgot all about it." Her stomach clenched at the thought of going to the academy instead of seeing Frank off at the station.

"Forget about it you should." Her father's voice boomed out. "You've a young man to take care of here. I'll go to the academy and tell them the class is cancelled for today."

"Thank you, Father." Amy gave him a hug. The clenching in her stomach loosened somewhat.

Amy clung to Frank's arm on the way to the train station. She kept her chin high, her gaze straight ahead, and a smile on her lips. She nodded to the townspeople they met on the way but didn't attempt to speak to anyone. She needed to keep her determination intact or she'd break down in tears before Frank left. That wasn't the way she wanted him remembering her when he was in Cuba.

Frank and Amy kept watch on the road, looking for his family. The Sterling wagon clattered into the train yard, the horses at a trot, only five minutes before the train was scheduled to leave. Jason and Andy were still in their field clothes.

Andy was the first out of the wagon. He ran up to Frank and shook his hand fiercely. "Sure wish I was going with you."

"Sure glad you're not," Frank shot back with a grin.

"I'll get there yet, you'll see."

Maggie and Grace embraced Frank, tears large in their eyes. Grace bawled outright when Pearl took her from Frank's arms.

"I was afraid we wouldn't make it in time," Jason said. "You never saw a team hitched up so fast." He pumped Frank's hand in a handshake and thumped him on the arm. "We'll miss you. Watch yourself."

"I will."

They stared at each other, continuing to pump each other's hands during the awkward silence.

They were only a year apart in age, Amy remembered. What must it be like to say good-bye to someone who's been part of your life for more than twenty years?

A whistle blew. A conductor called, "All aboard!"

Frank darted a look at the train and turned back to Jason. "Don't forget to pray for me."

"Every day."

Frank reached for Amy's hand and led her a few feet away. "I don't care what any of Chippewa City's old biddies say. I'm going to kiss you good-bye right here in front of anyone who wants to watch, Amy Henderson. If anyone has the nerve to say anything to you, you tell them they're only complaining because they're jealous."

His unexpected joking dashed her tears away from the surface.

He was as good as his word. He hauled her into his arms and kissed her long and hard, as if to make the memory of it last forever.

The whistle broke into their world. "Last call!" the conductor warned.

Frank loosened his hold and pressed his cheek hard against hers. She wanted to beg him to promise he'd come back to her, but she wouldn't allow herself to ask him to make a promise he had no way to know if he could keep. Her chest ached with the effort it took to keep the words to herself.

"You know I hate to leave you, don't you, Amy?"

She nodded, biting her bottom lip, and rested the palm of her hand against his chest. "Your beautiful heart is the reason I love you. I know you have to help those people."

He placed his palms on each side of her face and smiled into her eyes. "If I get back, Amy, meet me with a promise."

*If.* "What. . .what promise?"

"That you'll still marry me."

Her grin burst across her face, and joy and love flooded her. "I will. I will marry you when you get back."

With a lurch, the train started chugging along the track, the whistle blowing so loud that Frank yelled his last words. "Remember, I'll love you even if time stops!"

Then he ran for the train, grabbing the long handle beside the steps and jumping on board, the tin lunch pail swinging from one hand. He stood on the step and waved.

Amy watched and waved until the train was out of sight, all the time praying, "Bring him home to me, Lord. Bring him home."

❧

Five days later, headlines screamed, "Victory at the Battle of Manila." The people of Chippewa City were wild with rejoicing all day long and into the night.

Amy scoured the newspaper for knowledge of this war that had invaded her tiny prairie town, threatening the life of the man she loved.

The news came by way of Spain, whose government received the information by wire from Manila. Although President McKinley hadn't received word directly from the American officer in charge, he was convinced the report was accurate. "Why would Spain lie about losing the battle?" he asked.

A United States naval officer was quoted as saying the war would not be won with just the defeat of the Spanish soldiers on the ground at Cuba. He believed the Spanish fleet must be destroyed and, along with it, Spain's ability to access the island.

The United States under Commodore Dewey had attacked the Spanish fleet near Manila Bay on May 1, only days after Frank reported to the campgrounds at St. Paul. According to the article, all the Spanish ships in the Philippines were destroyed and many Spaniards killed. The United States lost no ships and only one man, who died of heat stroke.

Notes from Frank arrived almost daily. Amy treasured every one, although they were short and contained primarily mundane information about life at Camp Ramsey: new blue uniforms, living in converted stables on the state fairgrounds, training hours on end. His signature was always accompanied by a simple drawing of a watch face, which recalled to her his words, "I'll love you even if time stops."

Frank wrote that he was now part of the Thirteenth Regiment of Minnesota Infantry Volunteers. The long, proud name was soon shortened to the Thirteenth by Minnesotans and the press.

On May 17, Amy received a note in which the scrawled handwriting showed Frank's obvious haste.

*May 16, 1898*

*My dearest Amy,*

*I've only a moment snatched from packing to write this. We're mustering out today. The Thirteenth is heading for San Francisco. Please tell my family. I'll write when I can.*

*All my love always,*
*Frank*

The two other Minnesota regiments, the Twelfth and Fourteenth, had been mustered out to Camp Thomas in Georgia for further training. The Thirteenth was headed to Manila.

"I thought only navy men would be sent to Manila," Amy said to her father.

"Evidently the war secretary wants the infantry there, too."

The idea made Amy uneasy. "Do you think Frank will be safer in the Philippines than in Cuba?"

"Is any place safe in a war?"

The helpless look on her father's face only increased Amy's own helpless feelings. She fled to the riverbank where she and Frank had spent so many beautiful moments of their last afternoon together. There she poured out her fear and pain to the Lord.

After an hour or so, she allowed some peace to replace the distress she'd nurtured in her heart. She wiped away the last of her tears and heaved a shaggy sigh. "Lord, it seems since Frank left, not only words but every thought and feeling I have is a prayer."

At the end of May, President McKinley called for more men. Minnesota was ordered to raise almost another thousand to join the regiments already in the field. The governor put out a call for volunteers, as there wasn't another guard regiment available.

Chippewa City and the surrounding county created a

volunteer company. Young men left their families and farms and small-town jobs eager to prove their bravery and embark on the adventure of war with the men with whom they'd grown up.

Frank's sister Maggie started a group of girls who met every evening to make up linen bags for the soldiers. In the bags they placed a Bible, needles, thread, and a thimble. Amy thought it was a wonderful idea and joined the group whenever she could. She wrote Frank about the group, and he wrote Maggie, praising her efforts.

To Amy the country seemed turned upside down. Every train that came through town carried volunteers to St. Paul. Amy joined other young women from the Women's Christian Temperance League at the station, handing out cookies and coffee to the new soldiers who hung out the windows waving and grinning at their admirers on the platform. Along the tracks, children and young women and men waved scarves, handkerchiefs, and flags to cheer the soldiers on their way.

The town band sent the local volunteers off with renditions of the ever popular "Rally 'Round the Flag, Boys," as well as "The Star Spangled Banner," "Stars and Stripes Forever," and the romantic song too close to Amy's heart, "The Girl I Left Behind."

Maggie's group passed their linen bags to the volunteers, who accepted them with cheerful smiles.

Other scenes at the station were foreign to the sense of decorum with which Amy had been raised and seemed counter to the town's moral fiber. Young women met the trains with bouquets of early spring flowers and small budding branches and bestowed them along with kisses on soldiers, young men they'd never met or barely knew. There was a sense of the carnival about it all that lacerated Amy's heart.

She knew she wasn't alone in her pain. She saw it in the hooded eyes of mothers and fathers who sent their sons off to war. She witnessed a few couples who, like her and Frank, were deeply in love and hated to part. She relived the terrible sense of her heart tearing in two every time she saw such a parting.

Roland, the telegraph clerk who'd raced down the street with the notice of Frank's call to duty, joined the volunteers. Amy couldn't imagine jolly Roland in a battle scene. Petite, blond Sylvia saw him off at the train station. Tears filled the eyes of the usually bubbly girl. The couple often attended social events that Amy and Frank attended. The couple's friendship had grown slowly over the years into courtship.

Amy saw Andy at the station saying good-bye to friends and knew he wished he were joining the volunteers.

Slim and Shorty, the veterans of the War Between the States, met most of the trains, too. They cheered the new soldiers on. They recounted to anyone who would listen tales of the battles in which they'd fought. Amy was amazed how the two men, who had been enemies for years, now grew unified in their hatred of Spain. It saddened her that it took hatred and a common threat for the men to become friends.

The newspapers announced the first battle between the American infantry and the Spanish in Cuba had taken place on June 24. Amy's first thought was gratitude that Frank hadn't been part of it. Her second thought was shame and a prayer for those who lost loved ones in the battle—for the loved ones on both sides of the war.

It seemed eons before Amy received another letter from Frank, this one sent from Honolulu. He had started the letter the day he left San Francisco and continued it every day the ship traveled between California and Hawaii. Amy rejoiced over the length of the letter and the bits of his new life that he shared with her.

*June 27, 1898*

*My dearest Amy,*

*We left San Francisco today under General Arthur MacArthur. We sailed out of the harbor to a chorus of ships' steam whistles and guns. Flags and handkerchiefs flew from the shore and harbor.*

*We passed through the Golden Gate and on out to sea. That lady greeted us with winds and waves that made the prairie winds seem tame by comparison. Breaking a bronco is easy next to riding the Pacific's waves. I joined most of the others in a bit of seasickness, though it's nothing compared to my homesickness for you.*

He spoke of the long days on ship, the simple fare, and the heat.

*You never saw a thousand men so glad to put their feet on land as we were when we arrived in Hawaii. Took awhile to get our land feet. When we did, we swarmed through Honolulu's streets. The islanders presented us with wreaths made of flowers, which we wore like necklaces. The flowers reminded me of you and the floral fragrance you like to wear. I pressed a blossom in the pocket-size Bible I carry.*

*I'll send you a letter whenever I can, but I don't know when the next opportunity will arise. Know I am thinking of you every day and love you always.*

The familiar watch face adorned the letter at the end of each day's writing. Amy rested the palm of her hand over Frank's signature and imagined she touched the hand that wrote it.

She wondered if he knew that while he was in Honolulu, Congress had voted to annex Hawaii.

It seemed strange to think of Frank seeing parts of the world she might never see, experiencing sights and sounds and smells she might never experience. What did it feel like to sail the oceans, she wondered. What did the waves sound like against the hull of a ship? What did the flower wreaths that he said reminded him of her smell like?

Had he heard of the Battle of San Juan Hill in Cuba? Did he know that on July 16 the fighting in Cuba came to end with the signing of what were called "The Articles of Capitulation"?

The voyage took about a month. That would put him in the Philippines the end of July or perhaps the first week of August if the seas were rough or the stopover in Hawaii lasted longer than expected.

Amy felt as though she walked in a cloud of joy from the moment she heard of the peace in Cuba. Surely the troops in the Philippines would be sent home soon. "Perhaps Frank's ship will dock only to turn right around and come back," she said to her father.

"Time will tell."

The cloud darkened when an epidemic of typhoid fever broke out among the Minnesota volunteers in St. Paul in late July.

"I'm so glad Andy didn't join the volunteers," Pearl told Amy after a prayer meeting. "How awful to think of young men's lives threatened in camps on our own soil."

"Yes." Amy hugged her Bible to her chest. "Father says it's the same in every war."

"At least here we know the men will receive the best of care, with clean beds and enough medicine. Apparently the soldiers nearer the battlefields haven't that luxury."

"Doesn't it make you wish you could join Clara Barton and her Red Cross volunteers? It brought tears to my eyes when I read of their work with our men in Cuba."

"It takes a special kind of bravery to do what they do. I

admire them, but I know my place is here, taking care of my family."

"Yes, I'm sure you're right." *But I don't have a family to raise. There's only Father, and he doesn't need me the way Pearl's children need her.*

A chill ran through Amy when she read of another battle in the Philippines the night of July 31 and August 1. She scanned the article, frantic, until she'd assured herself the Thirteenth Regiment wasn't involved. On another page she saw a short article, only a paragraph long, saying the Thirteenth arrived in the islands August 1.

The hope and joy that had filled her upon the cessation of fighting in Cuba dissolved. She wished she were with the Red Cross, that she had the knowledge to help the wounded, that she was in the Philippines and could help Frank if he were wounded.

"But I don't have the knowledge, and I can't help anyone," she lamented to the Lord while seated along the banks of the river.

The flooding waters of spring had receded. The river no longer swirled angrily or hurled along whatever it caught in its path. The dark waters flowed peacefully, sun-dappled beneath the cottonwoods that shaded her. If only the country's angry flood had receded, too, she thought. She'd like to feel as peaceful inside as the river before her appeared.

"If there were only something I could do." She straightened. "Maybe. . .maybe I can help after all."

Two days later she entered Camp Ramsey. At the post hospital, she spoke with the officer in charge. "I have no training as a nurse, but I can sit with men who are ill. I can bathe their foreheads, help feed them, change their bedding, and pray with them. I don't care how mundane it is. I will do anything, just let me help."

The officer's eyes and cheeks were sunken with fatigue.

His gaze searched hers. "You don't know what you are asking. We are fighting a serious disease, an often fatal disease."

"I do know. That's why I'm here."

"Have you no one at home to care for?"

Amy removed her left glove and held out her hand. The tiny ruby flashed from her finger. "The man I love is with the Thirteenth in the Philippines. I only hope he has all the help he needs should he be injured or fall ill."

"He will most likely return. Most soldiers do." His smile barely touched his tired eyes. "You want to be alive when he comes home."

"I want him to come home alive. Every man in this camp has a mother or sister or loved one who wants him to come home alive, too. I want to help them."

They stared at each other across the desk. Amy forced herself to keep her gaze steady and her hands from trembling. She sent up a prayer that he would accept her offer.

He stood and gave a curt little bow from the waist. "Thank you, Miss Henderson. I will be honored to have you with us. I hope that man in the Philippines knows what a fine woman he has waiting here for him."

❧

The following days were the longest and most exhausting of Amy's life, but also the most rewarding. She helped with laundry, fanned and bathed feverish patients, prayed with them when they were frightened, held glasses of water for them when they were too weak to hold the glasses themselves, fed them, wrote letters to loved ones, read letters the patients received, washed dishes, cleaned lamp chimneys and trimmed wicks, and did anything else asked of her.

In every patient's face, she saw Frank's face. To every prayer for a patient before her she added a silent petition for Frank's safety. She experienced in a new way a sense of connection with all people through the Lord's love and learned in every painful place there is a blessing.

Amy's conviction that she'd made the right choice in volunteering solidified when young men from her county began appearing in the hospital beds. She spent time with each one, promising to take messages to loved ones if needed.

Hurrying about her duties, she spotted a familiar red-haired young man in one of the beds. "Oh, no, not Roland." It took her a couple minutes to compose herself before she could approach his bed with a smile.

She held one of his hands between both of hers. "Hello, Roland. It's Amy."

Feverish eyes opened. "Amy. Heard you were nursing."

"Helping out. I'm not a nurse."

His eyes closed. "Not supposed to be like this."

She leaned over to hear him better. "What isn't?"

He didn't answer immediately. She waited, sensing him gathering his strength to continue talking. "War. S'posed to fight, not get sick like this."

She smoothed back his hair, which was wet with sweat. "Rest, Roland. Spare your strength."

"Want to talk while I can."

"You have to believe you'll get better."

"Don't think that's going to happen."

"Would you like us to pray together?"

A minute passed before he responded. "Think God will listen to me? I've been living pretty rough."

Amy knew what he meant. Frank had expressed concern over Roland's drinking. The academy had suspended Roland for it. Frank had remained friendly with him, hoping to help his friend. "God knows none of us are perfect."

She sat at the edge of the bed, holding his hand. Her prayer was simple. At the end he joined her in an "amen."

His fingers gripped hers when she stood. "Can you stay a little longer?"

Duties called. She hesitated. "Of course." She sat down again and spoke of happy memories, times she and Frank had spent with Roland and Sylvia.

"If I don't make it, will you tell Sylvia I love her?"

The lump that suddenly filled Amy's throat made it difficult to answer. "Yes, but she knows it, Roland."

"Should have asked her to marry me. Tell her I wish I had."

"I'll tell her."

Another patient lay in Roland's bed when she came to the ward the next morning. Roland hadn't made it. Working the long day was difficult with the knowledge of his passing swelling her heart. Back at her own simple cot that evening, Amy wrote to Sylvia. The government would inform Roland's family of his death, and Roland's family would inform Sylvia. But the government wouldn't tell Sylvia of Roland's love for her.

Several of the patients, as they regained health, showed interest in Amy as a woman. When they did, she showed them her ring and spoke of Frank. To a man, they told her they hoped he would return to her.

One of the things the patients liked best was the little sketches she made of them and the camp on the letters she sent to their families. She took care the sketches didn't show the ravages of the disease. It filled a special place inside her to know that finally her talent, which had seemed so inadequate in this war, was being used to help others even in such a slight way.

Recalling the work of Frederic Remington and Howard Chandler Christy, who recorded the war in Cuba in sketches for *Harper's Weekly* and *Leslie's Weekly,* she made sketches of camp and hospital life and sold them to the *St. Paul Pioneer Press.*

She wrote Frank of her decision to volunteer at the hospital and described the humble tasks that made up her days. She had no idea when or if he would receive her letters, but she continued to send them.

Two weeks after Amy's arrival, Camp Ramsey reverberated with joy. Shouting and cheers and singing and gun salutes by the healthy volunteers marked the news that Spain and the United States had signed a peace protocol. That night Amy smiled as she said her evening prayers. She slept better than she had since Frank left for the war.

Two days later, she picked up a newspaper after a long day at the hospital and read that the day after the peace protocol was signed, the Thirteenth had fought its first battle at Manila.

# four

Frank grinned as he walked away from mail call. The mail had been a long time catching up with the regiment, but the letters from his brothers and sisters in addition to those from Amy made it worth the wait.

He dropped down beneath a palm tree, welcoming the shade, and placed the letters in the sand beside him. Pushing his broad-brimmed, high-crowned campaign hat back from his forehead, he picked up the envelopes and arranged them in the order post-marked. He was determined to read them in date order, though he was sorely tempted to read all of Amy's letters first.

He rubbed the palm of his hand over the beard he'd grown since leaving San Francisco and opened a letter from Andy. His younger brother had finally turned eighteen in August, but he hadn't joined up yet. He was waiting for the typhoid epidemics in the camps to pass before enlisting.

*Maybe he won't enlist at all,* Frank thought, *now that Spain has signed articles of capitulation in both Cuba and Manila.*

Frank opened the first letter Amy wrote in August, ignoring the man who sat down beside him until the man spoke.

"From that silly grin on your face, I expect that's a letter from your favorite girl, Sterling."

"You've got that right." Frank lowered the letter, only mildly annoyed at the interruption. Dan Terrell had become a good friend since they arrived on the Philippines. The two had fought side-by-side during the Battle of Manila, making their way through the city by ducking behind and climbing over garden walls and scurrying for cover beside native huts and wattled fences.

Frank pulled out his pocket watch, opened it, and handed it to Terrell.

Dan looked at Amy's picture and whistled appreciatively. "She's a pretty lady. How'd a guy with a face like yours get so lucky?"

Frank retrieved his watch with a grin and snapped the watch cover shut. "Charm. Need lessons?"

Dan chuckled, brushing from his forehead the brown hair that curled in the island's moist heat.

"How about you?" Frank asked. "You have a special lady waiting for you back home?"

Dan looked out at the thatch-roofed huts before them. "No. My lady died."

Frank was stunned into silence for a minute. "I'm sorry. I didn't know."

Dan nodded, still staring straight ahead.

Frank swallowed, trying to moisten his suddenly dry throat. "What happened?"

"Horse-and-buggy accident last winter. The buggy tipped over, and Belinda—that's my wife—her neck was broken."

His wife? "Were you married long?"

"Two and a half years."

Frank tried to imagine how awful it would be to lose Amy that way. Even the possibility of her death was too painful to consider. "Do you have any children?"

"We were expecting our first child when Belinda had the accident."

Frank's stomach tightened at the drawn look on Dan's face and the hollow sound of his voice. Frank couldn't think what to say to his new friend. A letter stuck out of Dan's shirt pocket. Frank indicated the letter with a wave of his hand. "Looks like you received news from somebody today."

Dan looked down at the envelope as if surprised at its existence and grunted. "From a friend." He drew it from his pocket, fingering the envelope as though undecided whether or not to open it. "Belinda and I rented his farm."

"Where was that?"

"Southeastern Minnesota, near Northfield."

"I'm from the opposite side of the state. Aren't you going to read the letter?"

"Sure." Dan tore the envelope open and unfolded the letter.

*Had he wanted to wait to open it, to draw out the experience?* Frank wondered. *Hadn't Dan received any other mail?* Frank cleared his throat. "Do you have any family back home?"

Dan didn't look up from the envelope. "My folks died from diphtheria back in '88. Had a sister and brother once, but they died when they were kids."

"My parents are dead, too." Frank glanced at his pile of letters and thanked God for his brothers and sisters.

Turning back to Amy's letter, he began reading it slowly, savoring every line as he had done with each letter before.

*I've envied the Red Cross nurses who helped the wounded in Cuba. Are there Red Cross nurses in Manila? I wish I were there, close to you. I wish I were a nurse and could help if you were injured.*

Frank was fervently glad she wasn't a nurse. The last thing he wanted was for her to be in a battle area.

*You've perhaps heard that typhoid fever is ravaging the Minnesota volunteers at Camp Ramsey. I've volunteered to help in the camp hospital.*

"What?" Frank shot to his feet.

Dan looked up at him. "Is there a problem?"

Frank had to try twice before he could make his voice work.

"It's Amy. She's. . .she's volunteering at Camp Ramsey, helping with a typhoid epidemic."

"Is she a nurse?"

Frank shook his head vigorously. "No."

He was aware that Dan rose and stood beside him, waiting for him to finish the letter. Frank scanned the page, his heart racing as fast as it had the first time he faced enemy fire.

"She must be one terrific lady to do that," Dan offered.

Part of Frank wanted to burst with pride that she would offer herself so selflessly. The rest of him felt nigh on to bursting with fear. How could she do this to them? What if she caught the fever and died? What if he made it home from Manila and she was no longer there to share his life? How could the life he went back to possibly be worth anything without her?

He dropped to his knees, the letter shaking in his trembling hand. He grabbed the pile of unopened envelopes. He tossed aside all but those with Amy's handwriting.

Dan squatted beside Frank. "What is it?"

"I have to see if she caught the fever."

It was now mid-September. The last letter from Amy was dated August 13. The irony of the date was not lost on him; the day he first experienced battle.

Amy had been alive that day. He tore the envelope open and scanned the letter. Only mundane news, wonderful everyday news of her chores at the camp, of plans to move the camp to Fort Snelling in an attempt to break the epidemic's hold, of her assurance she still hadn't contracted the disease and was as strong as ever. He skimmed past the lines over which he would normally linger, those telling of her love and how much she missed him.

He pawed through the unopened letters from his family. There were no envelopes postmarked after Amy's last letter. That made sense, since it took about a month for the mail to make it to the Philippines from the States. It didn't give him much comfort. Amy could be lying in a Fort Snelling hospital bed right now, her body raging with fever. Or worse.

He felt Dan's hand on his shoulder. "She was all right when the last mail was sent," Frank told him.

He drew up his knees and rested his arms on them, then buried his face in his arms. He was too afraid to even cry. *Keep her safe, Lord.* His silent prayer screamed inside his head. *Keep her safe.*

*Amy must have felt like this,* Frank realized. This was what the fear felt like for all the women waiting at home for the men they loved to return from the war: numbing, terrifying.

He picked up her last letter again. Hot fear twisted inside him like a living thing. He understood for the first time that when she wrote the letter, she hadn't known whether he was alive or not. And he knew he had to do the same thing for her that she did for him with every letter. He'd write her back, tell her how proud he was of her, tell her the everyday things of his life here in Manila, avoid the horrible aspects of war, tell her he loved her, and pretend he wasn't wondering every minute whether she was alive or dead.

❧

Amy breathed deeply of the pine-scented air in the large hall, which was decorated for the Christmas party at Windom Academy. "It's good to be back, Mrs. Headley."

The slender, thirty-year-old brunette beside her stepped back from the picture she'd just hung on the wall. "I do wish you'd call me Mary. You're an instructor here, not a student. I consider you a friend and hope you consider me one also."

"Yes, I do." Mary and her husband, the director of the academy, had become trusted confidants since Amy began teaching art there four years earlier. "I can't tell you how much I appreciate your husband offering me back my teaching position now that my volunteer work at the fort is over."

Mrs. Headley patted Amy's sleeve. "We're glad you came through your experience without becoming ill from the fever. It seems a miracle."

"To me, too, although I'm not the only person working with the patients who didn't contract the disease."

Mrs. Headley studied the painting hanging in a wide tortoiseshell frame on the wall. Amy fought the desire to leave and not look back, a desire familiar to her whenever someone examined her work for the first time.

"It's lovely," the verdict came. "A perfect companion piece to the photograph beside it."

"Thank you." Amy's gaze slid to the photograph, which also hung in a tortoiseshell frame. In it, a woman stood in a parlor, her eyes cast down, her stance and facial expression showing sorrow; a young man in army uniform stood in the open doorway, his arms outstretched toward the woman, his own face expressing his yearning to stay.

Amy hated the photograph. It spelled out her life all too well. Half the homes she entered had a copy on a wall. When Amy saw a copy hanging on the wall at the academy, her frustration boiled over. She'd immediately gone to her studio at the school and started the painting that became her response: a young woman with arms spread in welcome, joy shining from her face, and a returning soldier walking through the door with matching joy radiating from him.

Mrs. Headley held the door leading to the classroom hallway. "Have you heard when Frank will return?"

"No. When the guard was called last spring, the men were told they would serve for two years or the duration of the war. He may not be home for another year and a half."

"A pity. I know you and he would like to start your life together."

Amy gave her friend a quick hug. "Thank you for understanding and for your prayers. You needn't tell me you are praying for Frank and for me and for us as a couple. I know you are. It makes everything easier to bear, knowing you and others are carrying us in your hearts and prayers."

Amy pulled on her mittens as she left the building, walking down the steps and across the snow-drifted walk toward the ravine-spanning bridge that led toward town and home. When would Frank be back, she wondered. When would this awful war be over and Frank return?

❧

In spite of the peace protocol, the war in Manila continued after Christmas and into spring. The war was no longer against Spain but instead against the Filipinos who wanted to re-establish their own government. The days and weeks and months dragged by for Amy. The Thirteenth was finally relieved in March of its duty guarding the city of Manila against its own people.

"Does this mean Frank will be sent home soon?" Amy asked her father eagerly, looking up from Frank's letter.

His reply was the same as always. "Time will tell. Only God knows."

Frank's next letter didn't bring welcome news of his impending return.

> *My regiment was assigned to guard the railroad, which runs north of Manila, against the Filipino insurgents. Looks like I'll soon travel even farther from the city. Today I was reassigned to an expedition into the interior of Luzon, another island. Unfortunately this means I won't be sending or receiving mail for awhile. Know that I'm thinking of you every hour.*

The letter sent chills along Amy's arms. Her heart trembled at Frank's news, and she sent up yet more prayers. He didn't need to spell out for her that this was not a Lewis-and-Clark type of expedition. The soldiers would be trying to flush out insurgents.

On a bright, clear day in May when the people on the Minnesota prairie were rejoicing in the warmth of spring, Amy opened her apartment door to Frank's sister-in-law, Pearl.

"What a lovely surprise. Do come in. I'll put on the coffee pot."

Pearl stepped into the parlor. "No, no coffee."

Amy stared at her, puzzled. Pearl's face was pale, her eyes filled with pain.

Amy's heart swelled until it seemed her ribs must burst from the fear and dread. "It's Frank, isn't it?"

Pearl nodded. She licked her lips. "He's wounded."

"How. . .how bad is it?"

"We don't know. We've only received notice he's been wounded in action." Pearl spread her arms in frustration. "We don't know what kind of wound, or how serious it is, or if he's being treated in the Philippines or sent back to the States. We don't know anything. Jason is trying to find the answers."

Amy pressed the palms of her hands to her face.

Pearl slid her arms around Amy's waist and hugged her close. "I'm sorry, Amy. I'm so sorry."

Amy moved her trembling arms stiffly about Pearl's shoulders. "I. . .I want to be with him. I have to find him. He needs me."

Amy felt the warm moisture of Pearl's tears against her cheeks and realized in amazement that there were no tears in her own eyes. All she felt was the full yet hollow place fear had carved in her chest and stomach. "I need to do something to help him. There must be something I can do, somewhere I can go to help him. Where can I go?"

"Jason will find out. Until then, your love can be with Frank, Amy. Your love and prayers can be with him."

*If he's still alive.* The words flooded into Amy's mind. She shut her heart hard against them.

❧

Amy fought her fears for almost a week while Jason battled for information detailing Frank's condition. Each day Amy listened for the train that brought the mail and hurried to the post office as soon as she thought the mail might be sorted.

"You almost beat the train today," the postmaster greeted her on Friday. "There are three letters here for you from that soldier." He drew them from a mail slot and handed them to her.

"Thank you." It seemed to Amy her heartbeat drowned out her words.

"I heard about young Sterling getting wounded. I hope it's not too serious. He's a good lad."

Amy smiled her thanks. Turning, she hurried toward the door. On the outside steps she almost ran into Pearl.

Pearl glanced at the envelopes in Amy's hand. "Are any of those from Frank?"

"All of them. I haven't opened them yet." Amy didn't want to admit she was afraid she'd break into tears when she read the letters.

"I've come into town each day to check on the mail. Jason and I are too anxious to hear from Frank to wait the extra hours for any letters to be delivered at the farm. I'll be right back out."

Amy waited beside Pearl's wagon. The wagon bed and horses gave her a sense of privacy. Amy barely noticed the creaking wheels and harnesses of passing wagons or the dust that rose from horses' hooves and settled on her spring-green hat and gown.

She glanced at the envelopes in her hands, wondering which, if any, contained news of Frank's condition. "Oh, no," she whispered. Her heart sank to her stomach. The handwriting on one of the envelopes wasn't Frank's, but it was addressed to her and had his name in the return address.

Her fingers felt frozen. She stared at the envelope, wanting to know what news it contained yet terrified to know.

Pearl hurried up to her. "Only one letter from Frank for Jason." She held it up.

Amy looked at it. "Frank wrote it. It's his handwriting."

"Of course it is." Pearl frowned in puzzlement.

"This one's not." Amy realized her friend didn't understand the significance. *But she's never written a letter for a soldier who couldn't write his own.* Amy tore the envelope open slowly. The rip of tearing paper seemed ominous. As if by not opening it anything awful would be kept contained. If only it were that easy.

*May 12, 1899*
*Philippines*

*Dearest Amy,*

*It seems the war has really caught up to me. I'm glad to tell you I'm no longer on the expedition on Luzon. Unfortunately, that's because I'm in the Red Cross hospital. I met up with an insurgent and lost.*

*Don't be afraid for me, Amy. I'm wounded, yes, but I'll pull through. The doctors did their best work on me and the nurses are following it up with great care. So promise me you won't worry. I won't be able to get the rest the nurses insist upon if I think you're worrying.*

Amy's voice caught in a sob. She pressed the fingers of one hand to her lips. The sudden mist in her eyes made the words look wavy.

Pearl touched Amy's arm but waited silently for her to regain control. Amy's voice wavered when she continued reading.

*You might not hear from me for awhile. They're shipping me back to a fort hospital in the States.*

*You may have noticed the handwriting is easier on the eyes than my handwriting. One of the nurses, Miss Patchett, is writing it for me. She insists that rest includes not writing letters. I've insisted she put in this explanation. I've spoken to her about you so often she says she'd know you if she met you on the street.*

*Love,*
*Frank*

Amy searched in vain for the usual clock face. Frank must not have told Nurse Patchett to include it. The omission added to Amy's sadness.

Pearl grabbed an edge of the letter and scanned it. "He doesn't say where he was wounded."

"No."

"He sounds cheerful."

Amy folded the letter slowly. "He probably doesn't want to scare us." She'd met many patients like that at the fort. They wanted messages sent to their loved ones but didn't want to frighten them. The letters of those who died from the fever often sounded the same in tone as those of the soldiers who lived. The knowledge ignited a burning pain inside her. "He must be weak since a nurse is writing the letter for him."

"Maybe he wrote one of these other letters."

He hadn't.

The letter seemed to cheer Pearl and Jason and their family, though Amy wondered whether they simply tried to keep hope alive for her. Surely they knew, as she did, that if Frank's wound wasn't serious, he wouldn't have been sent to the States for treatment. Instead he'd have been treated at the Red Cross hospital in the Philippines and returned to duty as soon as he was considered able-bodied.

The news of Frank's wounded condition spread throughout the small town and countryside. People stopped Amy everywhere she went to ask about him and express their concern. Reverend Conrad and the congregation prayed regularly for Frank. Amy hoped Frank could feel all the love poured out for him.

She was relieved to finally receive a letter announcing he was back in the States. She tried to ignore the pang of fear she felt that the letter was written by another Red Cross nurse.

*You needn't play Florence Nightingale and come see me, Amy. No man likes to be visited by his lady love when he must play the invalid. I assure you the doctors and nurses here are giving me the best possible care.*

Sighing, she ran her fingers over the signature, wishing it were truly his. The watch face was again missing. She wished Frank had asked the nurse to draw it. Immediately she scolded herself. "Don't act so petty, Amy Henderson. It's enough that he's alive and that you've heard from him again. There are many women not this blessed."

But the longing remained.

# five

When spring quarter at the academy ended, Amy felt at a loss. She couldn't remember a time when her painting hadn't pleasantly filled her days. Now she paced the school's studio, staring out the windows at the prairie sky and picturing Frank in a hospital bed. The oil paints dried on her palette before she remembered to apply them to canvas.

Letters from Frank no longer arrived in bunches. He'd written often before he was wounded, even though the letters weren't mailed as soon as they were written. Now the letters dribbled in, at first weekly, then farther apart. The loving phrases that had brought color to her cheeks and joy to her heart were no longer included.

Amy told herself if Frank were writing the letters himself, they'd come more often and be more personal. She worried that he wasn't writing his own letters yet. She longed to visit him, but he continued to insist neither she nor his family travel to the hospital. Amy had to admit to herself that the cost of such a trip would be prohibitive, but she'd find a way to cover the cost if he wanted her with him.

Church, Bible class, Women's Christian Temperance meetings, and caring for the home she shared with her father weren't enough to keep her mind from worrying.

"Visit us at the farm," Pearl suggested when Amy complained to her after a Sunday church service.

"You don't need me underfoot." Amy slid the strings of her ivory lace reticule over her wrist. Fingering the frayed cuff on her yellow linen sleeve, she sighed. "I need some new dresses, but I hate to spend the money on a seamstress."

"You don't need a new dress, just a new cuff." Pearl examined the material. "That's not badly frayed. A bit of lace on each cuff should cover the wear nicely."

Amy lifted her brows in surprise. "Honestly?"

Pearl laughed. "Of course. Haven't you ever freshened up an outfit that way?"

"No. You know I don't sew except to stitch on buttons and mend hems, as you taught me." Amy tried to keep the impatience from her voice. Growing up, she hadn't thought about the new gowns the dressmaker made for her each season. She hadn't wondered what other women did when their clothes wore out. It made her ashamed to realize how little she'd understood the way most people lived. Since her father had lost his money in the depression, she'd gained respect for the discipline and ability to live on little means.

"I'll gladly teach you more. We can start with freshening this gown. Perhaps you have some lace at home you'd like to use on it. Otherwise you can purchase some. Bring it out to the farm along with the dress."

"I can't let you neglect your work for mine."

"I've no intention of neglecting my work. I'll show you what to do. It will be fun. We can visit while we work."

"I'm all thumbs when handling a needle. You probably can't understand that, since you're one of those amazing women who can look at articles about cute needlework items on the women's pages in the newspapers and know how to follow the instructions."

Pearl's laugh pealed out. "Quit pouting. Sewing takes practice, like everything else in life. Come out to the farm. Evening would be best. Harvest is starting, and my days will be filled from sunup to sunset."

"You don't help the men in the fields, do you?" The thought of petite, feminine Pearl doing the work of field hands shocked Amy.

Pearl's eyes danced with laughter. "We hire men to help with harvest. Our neighbor, Thor, helps, too. In return, Jason and Andy help with his fields. Feeding everyone keeps me and Jason's sisters busy."

"May I help?"

Pearl looked taken aback at the offer. "Why. . .certainly, if you'd like, but please don't feel you need to offer."

"I need to learn to be a farm wife for Frank."

Pearl nodded. "The days are long and hot. Wear something old and cool and bring a work apron."

"May I bring some food?"

"Just bring your willing spirit."

Amy started for the farm early the next morning but not early enough to beat the farmers to the fields. The men and their machines and horses and the crops were silhouetted against the pinkish-orange horizon. Dust rose behind her buggy from the dirt road and met the grain dust from an amber field under harvest.

"The men like to get into the fields while it's cool," Pearl told Amy when she arrived at the farm. "It will warm up soon enough as the sun moves higher."

Pearl unharnessed Amy's horse. Amy watched carefully and asked questions and did as Pearl directed her. Amy had never harnessed or unharnessed a horse before. She was determined to remember how to do it.

"I'll get Maggie to rub the horse down for you." Pearl turned toward the house.

Amy took her apron from the buggy seat and fell into step beside Pearl. "Don't you need Maggie's help in the kitchen?"

"The horse needs to be rubbed down before it's turned out to pasture for the day."

Amy sighed deeply. "I don't know anything about life on a farm. I don't even know how to rub down a horse. Why Frank wants to marry me is beyond my understanding."

"Because you are fine and beautiful, through and through." Pearl grinned and linked arms with Amy. "Rubbing down a horse is one of the easiest things to learn, but we'll let Maggie take care of it for you today."

The cheerful yellow-and-white-walled kitchen was already warm and filled with the smells of coffee, eggs, ham, and apple pie. Bread rose beneath clean muslin cut from a flour sack. Maggie rolled piecrust on the work table in the middle of the room. Grace stood at the iron sink, working away at the stack of breakfast dishes. The girls greeted Amy with smiles that made her feel hugged and welcomed.

Viola sat in the middle of the linoleum floor, banging two kettle tops together. Pearl nodded at her. "She's noisy, but at least I know where she is."

Seeing the attention focused on his little sister, Chalmers hurried over to kneel beside her. He tried unsuccessfully to convince her to exchange the noisy lids for an old wooden spoon.

Amy grinned. She loved the casual, busy hominess that was so different from the small, quiet apartment she and her father shared.

At Pearl's request, Maggie headed outside to take care of Amy's horse.

"Where would you like me to start?" Amy asked.

Grace turned, her hands deep in the dishwater. "Can she dry the dishes for me, Pearl?"

Pearl hesitated. Amy suspected Pearl had another chore in mind, but she agreed to Grace's request. The ten year old kept up a lively conversation about a new litter of kittens and the field hands. Amy gave the child her full attention and found herself sincerely interested in something other than her worry for Frank for the first time in weeks.

Amy liked working in Frank's home. It made her feel closer to him. She and the Sterling girls planned a party for

Frank's homecoming while they worked. Whatever his wounds, the doctors wouldn't release him until he was healed. He might need time to regain his strength, but a nice picnic where family and neighbors could welcome him home shouldn't be too tiring. In fact, they were sure it would prove healing.

At noon Jason, Andy, and the hired hands, hot and hungry, came into the farmyard. Jason and Andy led teams of horses to the barn.

The men washed up at basins set along a wooden bench on the porch. Long board "tables" had been set up for the men beneath some cottonwoods so they could enjoy their meal in the shade. The women moved about in a flurry, carrying food and pitchers and coffee pots to the table. While the men ate, the women hovered about the tables, filling each plate or cup as soon as it was emptied.

The quick wash-up had removed the worst of the dirt from the men's faces and hands, but it hadn't removed the aroma of hard work. It seemed to Amy the smells of grain, earth, sweat, and the kerosene used to keep flies and mosquitoes at bay drowned the smells of the food. From the men's comments, the food smelled as enticing to them as ever, maybe more than usual. Amy was amazed at the amount of food the group consumed.

She smiled, watching Chalmers and Jason together. The boy insisted on sitting in Jason's lap the entire meal. Chalmers told his father all about his day, augmenting his limited words with animated gestures and facial expressions. Jason's gaze was soft as it lingered on his son. Amy believed she could see the love in his touch when his large, tanned, calloused hands tousled Chalmers's soft, pale brown curls.

The sight caught at her heart and awakened a craving. Frank loved children. She longed for the day when she would see their son seated on Frank's lap.

When the men had finished the last of their coffee and pie, the horses were retrieved, and men and horses headed down the dusty road back to the field.

The women relaxed then, enjoying their own meal. The respite was over before Amy felt ready, but she cheerfully helped carry dishes inside and began to wash them.

Soon the entire routine from the morning started over in preparation for supper. The kitchen was hotter than in the morning. If the open screened windows and door helped, Amy couldn't tell it. Her scalp and clothes were damp from perspiration, as were Pearl's and Maggie's.

After the evening meal, the men went back to the field and the women once more cleaned up the dishes. Finally Amy and Pearl walked out onto the porch.

The windmill stood tall against the darkening twilight sky. The breeze turned the windmill blades slowly, sending out a continual creaking noise. Evening insects joined it in a chorus. Dozens of tiny birds dove and darted over a nearby field.

"What are those birds?" Amy asked.

"Swallows. They always appear this time of night in August."

The peace of the setting sun sank into Amy's bones and spirit. She leaned against a white wooden post and sighed. "The cool breeze feels good. I can't remember ever being this tired. Is your life always like this?"

"No." Pearl rested her hands on the railing beside Amy. "This is one of the busiest times of the year."

"That's good. I was beginning to fear I hadn't the stamina to be the kind of wife Frank needs."

"He needs the kind of wife who loves him, who thinks she is the most blessed woman on the face of the earth to be married to him. That's the kind of wife every man needs."

Amy thought Pearl looked very content after the long day. "That's obviously the kind of wife you are." She smiled. "I'm glad you're happy with Jason."

"I am." Pearl returned her smile. "I won't pretend this is the only busy time of year. We put in long days all spring, summer, and fall. Jason and the boys take care of the fields and livestock. The girls and I take care of the home, but I like the feeling that we're building this life together. I guess a lot of people think it's a hard life, but it's a deeply joy-filled life also."

Amy removed her apron and laid it over the railing. She repinned tendrils that had loosened from her topknot, then brushed ineffectually at wrinkles in her blue-and-white-striped work dress. *The day has taken its toll on my appearance,* she thought.

"I brought my yellow linen and the lace, as you suggested," she told Pearl, "but I haven't the energy to work on them now."

"One thing about mending, it can always wait." Pearl untied her apron and lifted it over her head. "This is the part of day I like best. When the chores are done, Jason and I like to step outside and just be still together, watching our little world."

Amy let her gaze rove over the farmyard and nearby fields. She imagined Frank standing with his arm around her shoulders, enjoying the quiet with her. How long before they stood together here? Each day that passed brought them closer to their life as man and wife. *Farmer and wife,* she corrected herself with a smile.

Maggie and Grace came across the farmyard together, home from walking the cows and horses in from the pasture. Jason and Andy walked into the yard from the drive and met the girls at the bottom of the porch steps.

Jason mounted the steps, nodded at Amy, and headed for the washbasins. "Chalmers and Viola asleep already?" he asked Pearl.

"Yes, I guess the excitement of all the people around wore them out."

Jason grunted. "Hardly see those two these days."

Grace stretched her arms high over her head and yawned. "I'm going to bed, too." She hugged Pearl, then Jason. Wrinkling her nose, she shook her head. "Ugh. You stink."

"I'll go in with you, Grace." Maggie opened the screen door. "I'm pretty well all in myself."

Andy followed Jason to the basins. "I'll hook up your horse and drive you into town as soon as I wash up here, Amy."

"Thank you, but I can drive myself back."

"No women leave our farm alone at night." Jason's tone left no room for argument. He kissed Pearl's cheek. "I'll be back when I'm done with the milking." At the bottom of the steps, he turned to look back. "Thanks for your help today, Amy. Mighty nice of you."

Andy bounded down the steps after Jason. "Should only take a few minutes to get your buggy ready, Amy."

Amy could barely see the brothers in the darkness as they walked toward the barn together. "I feel so guilty. They've had such a long day. Now Andy is looking out for me and Jason has to milk the cows alone. Some help I am."

Pearl rubbed her hand lightly on Amy's sleeve. "I'm glad you were here today. And Andy would rather drive you into town than milk cows, you may be certain."

Golden lamplight fell through the window and screen door, out over the porch, casting shadows. *Maggie must have lit a lamp,* Amy thought. Within minutes, moths softly thunked and fluttered against the screens. Smells of livestock and fields and trees washed away the clinging odors of the day-long cooking.

The sound of horses' hooves softly thudding on the drive caught Amy's attention. She turned her gaze toward where she knew the drive entered the yard. Two lit lanterns bounced in the dark, and she knew from their height that they hung on either side of a buggy. "Are you expecting someone, Pearl?"

"No. I can't imagine who it could be at this hour."

The buggy stopped in front of the house but too far away for the light from the kitchen to illuminate it.

"Hello," Pearl called.

There was no response.

The buggy lanterns revealed the shadow of one person, but the buggy top hid his or her features.

The person half-stood to get out of the buggy, and Amy could see it was a man. An excitement started, a stirring inside her. The man moved somewhat awkwardly as he climbed down, but there was something familiar about him, something—

"Frank!"

# six

Amy darted down the steps and over the path to the buggy, her heart racing, joy flooding her senses. She flung her arms around Frank's neck. "Frank! Oh, Frank, you're home. You're truly home." She pressed her lips to his cheek.

"Amy." The word was a hoarse whisper on the warm breath at her ear. His arm tightened about her waist, and he held her close against his chest. She felt him stagger slightly and step back under her fervent greeting. Guilt stabbed her. He'd been in a hospital for months. Naturally he'd be weak.

She loosened her hold, and he lowered her until her shoes touched the ground. Her hands rested on his shoulders. Even through the khaki shirt he wore she felt a difference. He'd lost muscle during his recuperation. Her heart trembled at the knowledge. *But he's home. With rest, he'll regain his strength.*

"What are you doing here, Amy?" Tension and confusion mingled in Frank's quiet question.

"Welcome home, Frank." Pearl's greeting awakened Amy from the world that included only her and Frank. She stepped back from Frank's arm to allow Pearl to greet him properly.

He couldn't have stopped at her home before coming here, Amy realized. If he had, her father would have told Frank she was here. As much as Frank loved his family, the Frank she knew would have come first to her. Why hadn't he let anyone know he was coming home?

An aching, tugging fear started in her stomach. She recognized it immediately as an extension of the fear that she'd tried to ignore for weeks—the fear that Frank was pulling his heart away from her.

Frank leaned down and touched his cheek to Pearl's. "How's my favorite sister-in-law?"

"It's so good to have you back."

"It's good to be back."

Watching them, unease tightened Amy's chest. Something was wrong. She wasn't certain what it was, but he didn't move like himself. Perhaps she was imagining it, reacting too strongly to his unexpected return. She frowned, watching him and Pearl. It was hard to see him clearly in the light from the buggy lanterns.

Running footsteps were quieted only slightly by the dirt as Jason and Andy came toward them, calling Frank's name. Before they reached the buggy, the back door slammed and Maggie and Grace joined in the race. A dog ran alongside them, barking as though he'd caught their excitement.

"Whoa." Frank gave a shaky laugh and stepped back against the buggy wheel. "I'm glad to see everyone, but I can't take you all on at once."

Laughter greeted his comment. Amy knew the laughter wasn't due to the humor as much as to their overwhelming happiness that he'd returned.

The family tossed questions at Frank.

"Did you get in on the last train?"

"Why didn't you tell us you were coming? We'd have met you at the station."

Andy pounded on Frank's shoulder in greeting. "You got here just in time to help with the milking. Sudsy's waiting for you."

Jason reached to shake Frank's hand. Grace dove in between the two men and threw her arms around Frank's waist. "I missed you."

Amy knew then, in an instant. The wound was to his right arm. She knew by the way Grace's arm pulled his khaki sleeve, the part below the elbow, tight against his body.

Grace gave a small cry and pulled back. "Where's your arm?"

Everyone stilled. In the darkness Amy could sense the horror and fear on the faces turned toward Frank.

*That's why he came home this way, in the night, without telling anyone. That's why he didn't stop to see me before coming here. That's why I've felt him pulling away from me. He was afraid we'd react just like this, as if he were. . .damaged.*

She slid her hand beneath his left arm and squeezed his arm gently. She pressed her cheek against his shoulder and looked into his eyes, trying to put all the love she could into her gaze. "I'm so glad you're back. I've missed you horribly."

The muscle beneath her fingers tensed. "I've missed you too." He looked at the others. "I've missed all of you."

A chill ran through her. He'd intentionally generalized the sentiment.

Her and Frank's actions stirred the others back to life. She heard a small gasp of a sob and saw Grace wipe tears from her face. Pearl slid her arms around the girl's shoulders and drew her back against her skirt.

"Well, you don't need to stand out here all night," Jason blustered with a cheerfulness that appeared false. "Come inside. Andy and I can take care of the horse and buggy. Rent it from the livery?"

"Yes." Frank didn't move.

Jason turned to Pearl. "Any of that coffee left? Must be some pie, too." He looked back at Frank. "Harvesting today. You know what that means. Lots of vittles."

Frank nodded.

"There's pie," Pearl assured. "The coffee is cold, but we can heat some up. The coals are still warm from the pies we baked this evening."

"Don't bother. Some milk would taste good."

"Say, we forgot the cows." Andy started toward the barn.

Amy thought Andy seemed inordinately glad to escape. He must have forgotten that he was about to drive her back to town, she thought. Or maybe he knew she wouldn't want to leave now or expected Frank to drive her back.

Frank tugged his arm gently from Amy's hands. He reached into the buggy and pulled out a leather satchel.

Jason grabbed the satchel handle. "I'll get that."

"I've got it." Frank's voice was tight but even.

Frank led the way toward the house, carrying the satchel. A sense of strangeness and loss swept through Amy. It was unlike him to walk on and leave her behind. *I'm acting petty. This must be horribly difficult for him, and I'm thinking only of my bruised feelings.* She took a deep breath and followed the others.

Maggie hurried ahead of Frank when they neared the door and reached to open it for him.

In the kitchen, Frank set the satchel down and took a deep breath. "Mmm. Home cooking." He pulled a chair out from the oak kitchen table and sat down. Grace sat beside him and Jason across from him.

Amy wanted to sit beside him, but he made no move to indicate he wanted her there. He didn't even look at her.

She gathered plates from the open cupboard, while Pearl sliced the pie and Maggie brought cold milk from the oak icebox.

"How are the crops?" Frank broke the tense atmosphere with a question for Jason. "Too dark to see much on the drive out."

Amy was sure Jason had kept Frank informed on crop conditions with the letters he wrote every few days, but now Jason answered as though he'd never mentioned them, his voice too cheerful.

"Wheat's great. No rain when it was in pollen. Not one hailstorm hit. Heads so thick you wouldn't believe and some as long as my forefinger. Running thirty-five bushels to the acre."

A hungry, jealous look passed over Frank's face. "What about the turnips? Get them sowed last month?"

Jason nodded. "Yep. Last week of the month, same time Dad always insisted we plant them."

Amy watched Frank while she worked. He'd always had high cheekbones and a slender face. Now the beard he'd grown couldn't hide that his cheeks were sunken. Gray circles made his eyes look deeper set than normal. His brown khaki military shirt hung on him. Her throat ached with the love she wanted to express to him, the assurances she wanted to give him that she loved him whatever his wounds.

Only the forks striking ironstone plates and moths plunking against the screens sounded while the family ate. Frank, who had been right-handed, used his left hand with more skill than Amy expected. *Of course, he's likely been feeding himself for quite awhile at the hospital,* she thought.

Amy remembered the meals earlier that day, the teasing and friendly banter. How different from this simple shared dessert.

It should be a joyous time, a time of rejoicing. Was it his attitude or hers and his family's that made it more a funeral than a celebration? She searched her mind and heart for a way to make his return what it should be, to make him understand they were all thrilled he was alive and home among them. Nothing seemed adequate.

"The neighbors all ask about you, Frank," Pearl said a bit too brightly. "They'll be glad to hear you're home."

Frank pushed the last bit of crust on his plate about with his fork. "Did you finish the harvesting today?"

"No," Jason answered. "I think tomorrow will be the last day. We'll move on to Thor's when we're done here."

Frank's chair scraped across the linoleum as he pushed it back. "I'm pretty bushed. If you don't mind, I'm going to turn in."

In an unintelligible jumble, Pearl, Jason, and Maggie assured him all at once that of course they didn't mind.

Frank picked up his satchel and walked across the large kitchen, toward the door to the steps that led upstairs.

Amy watched him, her heart racing. He couldn't leave without speaking to her, if only a few words. She couldn't bear it. She willed him to turn around with each step.

When he reached the door to the stairway, he set down his satchel, then reached for the brass door handle.

Pearl was up in a flash. "You'll need a lamp. I'll light one for you."

Amy pushed her chair back and hurried across the room. She knew the family was watching, that they would hear every word, but she was beyond caring. She wanted to fling her arms around Frank and hold him until he could feel her love passing between them.

Instead she reached for his hand. He shrank back a bit from her touch but not completely. Was he afraid to show rudeness to her in front of his family? she wondered. She folded her hands around his hand and spoke quietly. "I'm glad you're home. I hate the things you've endured, but I'm so glad you're alive and back with us. I love you."

Time seemed to stretch forever while she waited for him to respond. His gaze searched hers somewhat warily. She thought he grew more tired before her eyes. "I'm all in, Amy. Can we talk another time?"

"Of course."

He tugged his hand lightly, and she released it.

Jason came across the kitchen with a newly lit kerosene lamp, and he and Frank headed upstairs.

The ache in Amy's chest grew to enormous proportions. *He didn't say he loves me, not once.*

❧

Frank set his satchel on the floor beside the bed. A colorful, lightweight quilt protected the double bed, though the weather was too warm to sleep under it. Frank sat down on the bed with a grunt, while Jason set the lamp on an oak stand near the head of the bed. Along the wall opposite the bed stood the simple oak washstand, a linen towel hanging on the side next to Andy's razor strap, and a white galvanized bowl and pitcher on top beside Andy's razor.

Frank brushed the palm of his hand across his bearded chin. He didn't care for the beard, but he didn't trust himself to shave with his left hand.

Lace curtains waved gently at the open windows. The wonderful smells of a summer night on a Minnesota farm—smells of earth and animals that he'd missed for more than a year—drifted into the room. An owl hooted in the night. The windmill creaked background music.

"Room looks the same as it did the night I left."

Jason turned. "Not much changes around here." His Adam's apple jerked as he swallowed. "About the threshing tomorrow—"

Frank tried not to sigh. It exhausted him just to think about facing simple questions like this. He rested his right ankle on his left knee and tugged at his boot. "I don't think I'd be much help. I wear out pretty fast these days. Amazing how getting wounded takes the stuffing out of you."

"Sure. 'Course you'd be tired. Anyone would be."

Frank grimaced at Jason's stumbling.

"Uh, do you need help with. . .anything. . .before I head to bed?" Jason asked.

"No. I can get my clothes off. Takes a bit of jerking and twisting, but I can do it. Good night."

"Yeah." Jason walked slowly to the door and turned around. "What Amy said downstairs, that goes for me, too. I wish this. . .this. . ."

"I lost my arm. You can say it."

Frank and Jason stared at each other. They didn't break their gaze as Jason continued slowly, "I'm sorry, sorrier than I've ever been about anything in my life, that you lost your arm. If it had to happen to one of us, I wish it were me."

"Don't pity me." Frank's anger flashed full-blown and brought him to his feet.

Jason flinched and raised an arm in a swift motion as if to protect himself.

*Does he think I'm going to attack him?* Frank wondered, then reminded his brother, "I knew the risks when I enlisted."

"Yes, I guess you did." Jason lowered his arm. His shoulders drooped.

*He looks as weary as I feel,* Frank thought, so he tried to keep the anger from his voice as he said, "You'd better get some sleep. You've had a long day, and tomorrow won't be any shorter with all the harvesting."

Jason nodded and reached for the door handle. "I'm glad you made it back alive. I laid awake many nights fearing I'd never see you again, praying you'd come back." He raised his arms slightly and let them drop back to his sides. "Good night."

As Jason turned to leave, Frank thought he saw the lamplight reflect from tears in Jason's eyes. The moment was so brief that Frank wondered whether he'd imagined the tears.

Pity. The one thing above all he wanted to avoid, that he knew people would feel, that he didn't want them to feel for him.

He rubbed his eyes with his thumb and forefinger as he heard the door close gently behind Jason. *It's not true,* Frank thought. *It's not true that I knew the risks when I enlisted. I knew there was a risk I'd die and wouldn't be able to spend a lifetime with Amy. I thought if I made it back, I'd pick up my life where I laid it down when I left. I never thought I'd come back like this.*

The anger at Jason dissolved, leaving Frank even more

tired. He sat down on the edge of the bed. *I've bungled it badly. I should have written them about my arm. Shouldn't have sprung it on them this way.*

But each time he'd thought of putting it down with ink on paper, he'd panicked. Once the words were written, his loss would become too real. He'd be forced to face his fears about the way people would react, the fear that they'd stop seeing him as Frank and start seeing him as Frank-the-man-with-one-arm.

And there was Amy. He hadn't wanted her to have a chance for pretense, to pretty-up her reaction. He'd wanted to know her true and honest feelings. Maybe that had been unfair, but he wasn't sorry for his choice.

Leaning back against the pillows, he pulled his watch from his pocket. He pressed his thumb against the trip mechanism, and the cover popped open. His gaze lingered on Amy's image as he held the case near the warm lamp. With a sigh, he set the open watch down on the bedside table.

When he'd awakened in the hospital after the surgery on his arm, the first thing he'd asked for was his watch. He'd fumbled to open it. It had stopped.

He let himself relive the moment Amy recognized him, the joy in her voice, the way it felt to be in her arms again, the soft, eager kisses against his cheek. If he didn't experience anything else good for the rest of his life, he'd have that moment—the memory of her gladness at seeing him again.

It would need to be enough.

❧

Amy stared out her bedroom window at the dark, shrub-covered hillside behind the building. She released the lace curtains she'd been fingering and hugged herself, sorrow overflowing in tears but never lessening.

The room was dark. Clouds covered the moon. Amy's heart felt as devoid of light as the world about her.

She hadn't known it was possible to hurt this much. For

over a year she'd longed and prayed for Frank's return. Now he was home. Or was he?

It was as though he'd built a wall between them. She saw the wall reflected in his eyes, felt it in the way he drew back from her touch. Had he stopped loving her? She'd always heard that absence made the heart grow fonder, but Frank's absence appeared to have separated them not only in body but in heart.

Tears fogged her view through the window. She drew a shaky breath and moved to the bed, fingering the button at the collar of her white shirtwaist.

*I should wash up and change into a nightgown,* she thought, *but I'm so weary.*

She lay down on the old pink satin comforter. The faint scent of lavender rising from the lace-edged pillowcases didn't hide the cooking odors still in her hair and clothing. She twisted a tendril that had come loose from the topknot earlier that day.

"Oh, my." Realization stilled her finger. Dismay swirled through her stomach. She hadn't thought until now what a mess she'd been when she greeted Frank. As much as she wished she'd looked her best for him, she knew his distance wasn't caused by her mussed hair and rumpled, sweaty blouse and skirt.

"I don't think I can bear it if he no longer loves me, Lord," she whispered into the darkness. She tried to picture the future without Frank and couldn't see a future. "Let him still love me, please." She wanted to repeat the prayer and repeat it again, then again, as if repeating the request would increase the likelihood God would answer as she wished.

*If we'd married before Frank left, he would have come home to me instead of the farm. I could have held him and surrounded him with love, maybe enough love to absorb his pain or at least to lessen it.*

What but love—hers, his family's, and his friends'—could

help ease the pain and fear of learning to live without his arm? He was obviously pushing away her love and his family's. Was he pushing away God's love, too?

*Please heal his heart, Lord.*

In the face of Frank's pain, the other prayer her heart persisted to cry out—that God would keep Frank's love for her alive—seemed selfish.

She yearned for sleep to come and anesthetize her fears, but it didn't. She turned her mind away from her fears and chose instead to remember the moments beside the buggy when she and Frank held each other close, and there was nothing in her heart but joy, thanksgiving, and great love.

# seven

Frank laid back in the tall prairie grass beside the pond and breathed deeply, luxuriating in the scent of wild grass, prairie flowers, and earth. He stared into the cloudless morning sky and felt his heart almost burst in gratitude that he was back in the place he loved best, back in a place of peace.

He shifted his broad-brimmed felt hat over his forehead and closed his eyes, sighing in contentment. Here no one would order him to shoot someone. Here he needn't dodge bullets or swords. Here he needn't quiet his breathing to hear whether the enemy was near. Here he could relax amid the medley composed of the chirping of crickets and grasshoppers that crawled benignly over him, booming prairie chickens that hid beneath the waving grass, croaking toads on fallen logs, and warbling red-winged blackbirds that bounced on pussy willows at the pond's edge.

He felt rich amid the ordinariness of the prairie.

Abruptly his hat lifted, and rays from the early morning sun fell full on his face. His eyelids flew open.

His brown hat dangled inelegantly above him from the mouth of his favorite cow. He grabbed for the hat, his laughter ringing out. "Sudsy, you remember our game."

Frank stood up, settled his hat back on his head, and rubbed Sudsy behind one ear. With a sigh, he started back to the farmstead, the tall grass bending beneath his boots.

He was entering the barn when he heard horse hooves, the creak of a harness, and the rattle of wheels. He turned to see who was driving into the yard. Amy.

For a moment, he felt frozen to the spot. Impulsively, he stepped into the barn. Maybe she hadn't seen him.

He took a deep breath, closed his eyes, and clenched his fist. This was ridiculous. As much as he wanted to hide in the dark depths of the barn from the rest of the world, he couldn't do that forever. "Might just as well get used to facing people right off."

No one he'd rather see less at this moment than Amy. "Probably why she's here," he muttered, opening the heavy door. "Some sense of humor You've got, Lord."

Amy was already climbing down from the buggy, her back to him. She steadied herself with one hand, while the other hand held the skirt of her blue-and-white-checked cotton dress out of the way.

He stepped up behind her. "Let me help you." He reached to grasp the elbow of the arm with which she clutched her skirt.

He missed as Amy gasped and turned her head quickly to look over her shoulder. "My, you startled me."

He reached for her elbow again to steady her, and this time he succeeded. Memories of the many times he'd helped her from buggies and wagons, often catching her to himself with both arms for a stolen kiss, filled his chest with painful longing. The gentle floral scent she wore increased his awareness of her. Her straw hat, decorated simply with a ribbon that matched the pale blue in her dress, hid her face while she watched her step.

As soon as Amy stood steadily on the ground beside him, he released her elbow.

"Thank you, Frank." She looked up at him, her green eyes searching his face. Was she wondering why he hadn't sought her out last night?

Uncomfortable under her scrutiny, he shifted his weight and peered into the buggy. "Anything in here you need?"

"Only the aprons that are lying on the seat."

He stepped up, balancing carefully, and reached for the aprons. A wooden easel caught his attention. When he handed her the aprons, he indicated the easel with a jerk of his head.

"Why did you bring your painting things?"

"They're still in the buggy from yesterday." Amy's gaze darted away, and she shook her head, laughing softly. "Yesterday was my first day helping during threshing. I've been wanting to paint a field scene and thought I might have time yesterday in between rushes of work. I'm sure you know how mistaken I was in the belief there'd be empty time to fill."

He chuckled, genuinely amused at her sweet innocence and ignorance of farm ways. Almost immediately followed a sense of surprise that she'd so soon and easily slipped under the barricade he'd set up against her.

Quickly, he reached for the driving rein. "I'll take care of your horse. You can go on up to the house." The words came out in a harder tone than he'd intended. *Perhaps that's best,* he thought.

"Pearl showed me how to unharness yesterday. I can help you."

"I don't need your help." Anger sprang up with the quickness of lightning. It was bad enough he wasn't carrying his share of the threshing. "I don't need help from a woman to unharness a horse and rub it down. I've been doing this since I was knee-high to a grasshopper."

Amy looked as if he'd struck her.

He pressed his lips together hard to keep back the apology that leaped from his heart and turned to his work. She'd accept more easily what he had to say later if he allowed this wound to fester.

After caring for Amy's horse, Frank sat in a pile of fresh straw inside the barn. Rubbing down a horse had never wearied him this much before. He could hardly keep his eyes open.

The sound of the draft horses from the field being led into the barn awakened him. He stood up almost before he was fully awake, not willing to be caught sleeping by his brothers or by any of the others who'd spent the morning working hard in the fields.

He stepped around the end of a stall and saw Andy and Jason with the horses. "Need a little help there?"

His brothers glanced at each other, then at him. He understood that wary look. "I can rub down a horse and give it feed and water."

"Little help would be nice," Jason said evenly.

Frank found his will was stronger than his body. His nap hadn't restored the strength lost from his work with Amy's horse and the walk to and from the pasture with the cows. He was acutely aware that he performed far less than one-third of the work. By the time the brothers were ready for dinner, Frank's shirt and hair were soaked with sweat.

His heart beat wildly as he followed his brothers out to the planks-on-sawhorses tables where the workers had already finished their main meal and started on the pies. He grinned. *Haven't been this nervous since I first asked Amy to allow me to court her.*

He'd just as soon avoid meeting Thor and the hired workers—many of whom had worked the Sterling farm for years—but he figured he might as well get it over with. Have to happen sometime. Besides, if he was going to stay jittery about letting people see him with only one arm, he'd need to become a hermit.

*The idea has its merits,* he thought, watching heads swivel to face him.

Greetings poured forth from the gathered friends before Frank reached the washbasins on the back porch. He grinned, feeling self-conscious. "If you don't give me a chance to wash up, you better sit upwind of me, folks."

They laughed and allowed him time for a lick-and-a-promise wash job.

When he returned to the table with his brothers, the welcome-homes started all over. He nodded and smiled and shook hands awkwardly with his left hand as he walked toward an empty seat. He seated himself and began to fill his plate from the serving platters and bowls the women had replenished. "Sorry I'm not joining you fellas in the field today. Hate to seem a slacker. I'm mostly back to snuff but still wear out pretty quick."

Shifting bodies and ducked heads revealed the group's unease at his oblique reference to his injury.

"You weren't a slacker serving yer country," the bulky man beside him said fiercely.

"You betcha." Swedish Thor from the neighboring farm bobbed his head in agreement.

"This time next year we won't be able to keep up wit' you," a bald Norwegian across from him asserted.

Frank's heart warmed to their desire to make him feel normal and comfortable, though part of him held to resentment that, like his family, they appeared trying too hard to act cheerful and ignore his arm.

Pearl set a golden-crusted pie on the table. "Guess a war hero has a right to rest a bit." Her chin stuck out in belligerence, and her eyes flashed, challenging the men to contradict her.

"I'm hardly a hero." Frank dropped his gaze to his plate and stuffed a forkful of mashed potatoes into his mouth. Why did women say such fool things? He thought his sister-in-law was wiser than most about the things that hurt a man's pride.

"You are to us." Thor's soft Scandinavian accent didn't hide the sincerity behind his words.

"Lemonade, Frank?"

His heart skipped in surprise at finding Amy beside him with a creamy porcelain pitcher in one hand and a glass in the other. There was a small smile on her lips and question in her eyes. He sensed the question was more about what he felt toward her and how he would react to her than about lemonade.

"Lemonade would hit the spot, thanks."

He allowed himself to study her while she poured. The heart-shaped ruby in the ring he'd given her flashed in the sunlight. His heart crimped at the memory of the many dreams that ring represented. A white apron with ruffles and a couple small kitchen splotches now covered the blue-and-white-checked gown. He found it unexpectedly endearing to see her at his home looking so housewifely.

The domestic term frightened him. He couldn't allow himself to imagine her part of his everyday life in such a homey and wifely manner. He yanked his gaze from her.

Thor grinned. "When are you two hitching up?"

Even Frank's ears heated at the question. Hired hands watched with curious and laughing eyes.

Frank jabbed his fork at a piece of meat. "We haven't had time to discuss it. I only got back last night, you know."

"Better get her to the altar fast." Thor's advice was given with a laugh in his voice. "There are a couple young men in town itching for a chance to court her. They've held back out of respect while you were away serving your country, but if you don't marry her soon, you'll have a fight on your hands for her." Thor's eyes danced beneath his shaggy gray-blond brows.

Frank forced a grin and wondered what Amy, who still stood beside him, was thinking.

Amy's soft voice interrupted the laughter. "You might tell your friends that Frank Sterling is the only man for me."

Laughter erupted again as Amy moved to the next man to offer lemonade.

Guilt twisted Frank's heart, though he continued to grin to keep up the charade. To avoid facing Amy or the others, he gave his attention to pouring gravy over a second helping of potatoes. *When I was in the Philippines, I thought life was going to be easier if I ever returned home. Instead, I'm just dodging bullets of another kind.*

❧

Frank spent the afternoon alternately wandering familiar pastures and the edges of fields and taking catnaps, sometimes in the barn and sometimes in a fragrant, shady spot outdoors. He avoided the farmyard where the children played and the house filled with womenfolk. It distressed him that he fatigued so easily from such little physical effort. By suppertime, his shoulder and arm ached.

He joined the others for supper, finding it easier to face the group the second time. After the meal, the men went back to the fields to steal a couple more hours of work from the day. The women went back to the kitchen to clean up the dishes. Maggie and Grace went to the pasture to bring the cows back.

Frank sat beneath the maple tree. A small breeze had come up, rustling the leaves above him and chasing away the mosquitoes. He scratched the golden tabby cat in his lap. "Good old Gideon. I was gone so long I was sure you'd forget me. Old faithful, that's you." The one-eyed cat stretched its neck and kneaded Frank's thigh. "At least I know you don't care that I came back slightly the worse for wear."

He leaned his head back against the tree trunk and sighed. He'd told Amy they'd talk this evening. He dreaded that talk. "I'm going to need some help, Lord. It's going to take all the courage I can muster; a whole lot more courage than it took to go to war."

"What will take more courage than going to war?"

He started at Amy's question, and Gideon jumped from his lap. "I didn't hear you come up."

"You said you wanted to talk with me after supper."

"Yes." He stood up.

"So, what will take so much courage?" Amy repeated, smiling up at him.

He recognized the guard she put on her smile and knew it was caused by his abrupt attitude toward her thus far. With a sinking sensation in his chest, he realized that after this talk, he might never again receive the smile of complete welcome he was accustomed to from her.

# eight

Amy clasped her hands together behind her. She was glad she'd bolstered her own courage by washing her face, straightening her hair, and dabbing a bit of Pearl's violet water to her wrists and neck.

She tried to hide her nervousness from Frank with a smile. He looked altogether too guilty for her comfort. "Apparently you intend to keep that object of courage a secret."

Frank hooked his thumb in his trouser pocket and rested his shoulder against the tree trunk. "It was nice of you to come out and help Pearl the last couple days."

"I'm glad to do it. Besides, I've so much to learn."

He frowned. "About what?"

"All the things a good farmer's wife needs to know." Amy spoke lightly, hoping to disguise the fear that caused her throat to feel as if her heart were lodged in it.

He took a deep breath.

Her fear multiplied.

"Amy, I don't think we should marry."

Her stomach tightened. "Why?"

"I'm not the man I was when I asked you to marry me."

Hope surged through her. He hadn't said the words she'd most feared. He hadn't said he no longer loved her. "You mean because of your arm? Surely you don't think something like that could change my love for you." Impulsively, she stepped closer to him and rested the palm of her hand on the front of his shirt. She could feel his heart beat. "It's your heart I love. Losing an arm can't change your heart."

"Don't be too sure."

His sharp tone jerked her gaze to his eyes. Their usual

brown color looked black with emotion.

"War does change people, whether they're wounded or not."

"But—"

"I don't know what my life is going to be like from here on out. I don't even know whether I'll be able to support myself, let alone a wife and family."

"Other men do, men like Slim. Well, Slim doesn't have a wife and family, but he has a job."

"He's a store clerk."

She couldn't suppress a smile. "Aren't store clerks as respectable as farmers?"

"The job's not as physically demanding."

"I know it will take time to learn to do things with one hand." She raised her gaze to his and gentled her voice. "I'll wait as long as you feel you need, but I would rather marry soon. People who love each other need to be beside each other at times like this."

"You don't understand." His voice was as quiet as hers had been.

The fear that hope had routed only a minute earlier gripped her again. Since she threw herself into his arms when he arrived the night before, he hadn't hugged her. He hadn't kissed her once. Even now he hadn't touched her.

"I'm not asking to postpone the wedding, Amy. I'm saying I'm not going to marry you."

"But I told you, it doesn't make any difference to me that you lost your arm." Her fingers clutched his shirt.

"It makes a difference to me."

"You know that I mean it doesn't make any difference in how I feel about you."

"And I mean that it makes a difference in whether I want to marry you."

The conversation was spiraling out of control. Amy took a deep breath, but it barely lessened the panic in her breast. "If you'd lost your arm in a farming accident or even in the war after we married, you wouldn't expect me to reject my vows or stop loving you, would you?"

"There's no sense imagining situations. We have to live with life as it is."

Amy could barely hear herself think for the roar fear made in her ears. She pressed her fingers against her temples and stared over Frank's shoulder, trying to bring clarity to her thoughts.

"Amy, I'm sorry, but it's for the best."

She wanted to slip her arms around his neck and hug him close until he admitted he still cared for her, that it was only his silly fears that made him change his mind about the wedding. How could she hug him when he was trying to push her out of his life?

She lowered her hands. Her gaze searched his. "You haven't said you no longer love me."

He continued to meet her gaze evenly.

Her heart regained its equilibrium. "You *do* still love me."

"It wouldn't be loving to marry you now. You'd be marrying a stranger. I told you, I'm not the same man who left here over a year ago. I don't want you to marry me, then discover you don't love who I am now. What if you found you didn't love me and stayed with me out of pity or duty? You deserve a better life than that."

She didn't believe he wasn't the same person, but he kept insisting it was so. She studied his face, looking for answers she couldn't find. "Do you think it is noble to give up our dream of a life together?"

His gaze didn't falter, but he didn't answer.

"You do think it's noble." The knowledge sent anger pouring through her veins. "I don't think it's noble. I think it's horrid that you are turning away the greatest thing, the only thing, I have to give."

How could she convince him their love was strong enough

to survive his wound? Her mind was too filled with pain and anger to think clearly. The realization she was shaking increased her frustration. "If this is what you choose, there's nothing left to say."

"It's what I choose."

The soft, even tone chilled her as much as his words. "Good-bye then."

She started toward the house to collect her things. After half a dozen steps, she turned around. Frank was standing where she'd left him, watching her as she'd known he would be. "I guess you've changed after all. The Frank Sterling I know would never have walked away from us. He was convinced through and through that God meant us to be together, that we were God's gifts to each other. The Frank Sterling I know believed in us. He would have slain dragons to keep us together."

He simply stared at her with those dark eyes and the look other girls had called brooding when they were in school. She'd always felt she could read his heart in his eyes. Now he wanted to keep her out of his heart and its secrets.

Amy whirled and headed for the house again. Andy opened the screen door when she reached it. She gave him a large smile. "Would you have time to hitch up my buggy?"

"Sure, glad to do it. I can ride into town with you, too."

"Thank you, but I don't think that's necessary."

Andy smiled. "I forgot. I suppose Frank will be driving you home."

"No, but it's not dark yet. The sky is clear, and the twilight should be bright enough for me to drive safely." Amy was glad it wasn't dark yet. It would be mortifying if she started crying in front of Andy on the way home.

She kept her smile in place as she hurried through the warm kitchen, still redolent with baking and cooking odors, past Pearl, who was putting away dishes and pans. Her face felt tight with her smile, and her eyes wide and hot with tears that wanted to escape.

In Pearl and Jason's bedroom, she retrieved her hat. She turned to the mirror but barely noticed her reflection as she positioned the hat on her head. "Ouch."

"Did you hurt yourself?" Pearl's anxious question broke into Amy's jumbled thoughts.

"Stuck myself with the hat pin." Amy placed the pin properly on her second attempt, though it took an effort to control her shaking fingers. She smoothed her hands over her hips, hoping to keep the shaking from Pearl's notice. "There, I think I'm ready to go now."

Pearl gave Amy's shoulders a gentle squeeze. "What's wrong? Did you and Frank argue?"

Amy didn't want to answer. To put Frank's decision into words might give it life. But Pearl was her best friend, and likely Frank would tell her and the family of his decision soon anyway. Had he told them already? "He doesn't want to marry me."

The shock on Pearl's face assured Amy that her friend hadn't known of Frank's decision. "He can't mean that, Amy. He's loved you for years. You're the only girl he's cared for in his entire life."

"Nevertheless, he insists he won't marry me."

Pearl's arms enclosed Amy in a hug. "He's just upset about. . .about his arm and all. He'll change his mind when he's feeling better. I'm sure he will."

Amy held tightly to her friend. "I hope so." The words sounded thick with the tears Amy struggled to suppress. "Will you walk out to the buggy with me? I don't think I can speak to Frank now should he still be there."

"Of course."

Amy picked up her ecru lace reticule from the bed and slid its strings over her wrist. In the kitchen she retrieved her dirtied aprons from the wooden peg beside the door. She wished good night to Grace. Then she stepped quickly through the doorway onto the porch. She wanted to escape into a solitary place and examine her conversation with Frank piece by piece. Perhaps she'd missed something. Perhaps she could find a way back for them.

Relief and regret mixed within her when she saw Frank still standing under the maple. She turned her gaze from him and walked quickly beside Pearl to the buggy.

"He's all ready for you." Andy patted the horse's neck. "If you want to wait for a few minutes, I can drive into town behind you. We forgot all about returning the buggy and horse Frank rented from the livery last night."

"That's a kind offer, but I think I'll start out right away." Amy was glad no one was insisting on driving back in the buggy with her. "It's nice to know that you'll be coming along behind me soon in case I have trouble, though."

Pearl gave her another hug. "I'll be praying."

Amy hugged her tighter, surprised to find she didn't want to let go of this friend who cared about her pain. She recognized the gift in holding someone now that she was deprived of hugging Frank.

She drew a shaky breath and released her friend. "Do you need my help tomorrow?"

"No. The men are done here for the time being. Tomorrow they start on Thor's farm."

"I'm sure Frank will find that a relief." So did she.

She refused to allow herself to look toward Frank when she directed the horse toward the drive. As she left the farmyard behind, it felt as though she was leaving the only whole and unhurt part of herself behind as well. The woman she took with her was only shards of the woman who had waited all these long months for Frank to return from war.

❧

Frank leaned against the tree and watched Amy ride off down the drive in the twilight. It felt as though someone's fist was wrapped around his heart. "I'm not sorry," he whispered. "I'd do it again in a minute. She'll be happier this way in the end."

She deserved a whole man, a man who could support her well. One day she'd see that for herself. He'd rather it wasn't as his wife. He couldn't bear the thought of someday looking into her eyes and seeing, instead of love, distaste or pity or resignation.

He could still see the pain and disbelief in her eyes when he'd told her he wouldn't marry her. Her pain had sliced into his heart. It had taken all his strength not to take back the words, not to catch her close and say nothing on earth could ever make him leave her.

*It hurts her now, but she'll get over that.* He brought his hand to his chest. *I'll get over it, too, one day. Hearts don't really break.*

*Yes, they do,* a thought slipped through.

But it couldn't be true, because he could feel his heart beat. It was as strong now as the day he was born, though his heart felt crushed.

*We'll get over this. When we're sixty and gray-haired, we'll run into each other at the general store or church and smile when we remember how once we thought we couldn't live without each other.*

"But for now, please help her, Lord. Help us both."

❧

The men moved along to Thor's farm with the jointly owned threshing rig the next day, but there was still work to do in the Sterlings' fields. When Jason and Andy headed off to the neighboring farm, Frank headed to the Sterlings' oat field and began tipping shock butts to the sun to dry out the dampness from the ground.

Like most fieldwork, the chore had always been time consuming and tiring, but his muscles had mostly been up to the work from the time he was a boy. Today he started out with every muscle in his body screaming, already worn from yesterday's toll.

He forced himself to work through the pain. He was glad

for a chance to experiment with different ways of handling the shocks before working in front of his brothers' and others' eyes. After a bit of trying, he found he could use the top of his short arm to help balance the shock and do the work of turning with his hand. The first time it worked, joy jolted through him. He'd done it!

The joy remained through the next hour, but it became a calmer joy. His muscles continued to protest as he pushed them to obey his urgent need to become a useful member of the family again. He kept checking the height of the sun, wondering whether it had always moved so slowly in its path across the sky.

He stopped earlier than usual for the cheese, bread, and apple lunch he'd brought out to the field in a tin pail. His body insisted on the nourishment. He took some powders for the pain in his arm, washing them down with a drink of water.

The sun was barely halfway to its noon height, and already his shirt was soaked with sweat. He was tempted to remove it, but he hadn't kerosene with him to keep away the bugs. Not caring to become their lunch, he kept his shirt on.

Satisfaction filled him with sweet calm when he looked on the shocks he'd tipped. He went back to work with his energy slightly restored but his muscles still protesting. Now that he had the hang of tipping the shocks, his mind wandered more often from his work. Its destination was always Amy.

Fatigue and pain drove him home from the field earlier than in the past. He barely had energy to wash up before climbing the stairs to his room and throwing himself across the quilt-covered bed. His last thought before falling asleep was that, if God especially blessed him, his dreams would be free of the girl he loved and the pain of separation from her.

❧

Frank left the noise of wagons, buggies, and horses behind and entered Dr. Strong's pharmacy with Pearl. He'd only been home a week, but that short time working in the fields had been rough on his weakened muscles. Hope for relief brought him to the doctor. He left Pearl at a display of kerosene lamps near the front of the store and proceeded toward the back of the shop and the door to Dr. Strong's adjoining office.

*It's almost as much a general store as a pharmacy,* he thought with amusement as he passed a glass display counter with dainty porcelain gift boxes. Shelves filled with jars of every shape and size—clear, opaque, or clay—lined the walls behind the cabinets. Flowing black script on the jars identified herbs, salves, and other remedies.

A small wooden sign on the office door announced a patient within. A short oak bench beside the door invited him, as the next patient, to wait in relative comfort. Frank chose to browse the store instead.

He stopped short at the sight of Amy. She stood in front of a shelf of shaving mugs, her back to him. He wobbled between speaking to her or going back to the bench and hoping she wouldn't see him. He longed to talk with her, if only to hear her voice again, but how would she react? He hadn't seen her since their confrontation at the farm last week.

Talking with her won the battle. He removed his broad-brimmed brown hat. His boots sounded loud to him as he crossed the wooden floor, but she didn't turn around. He stopped behind her and cleared his throat.

"I'd like this mug, please." She turned around with a large porcelain shaving mug in her hands and a friendly smile on her face. The smile froze when she saw him. "You."

"Morning, Amy."

"I thought you were the clerk. I'm buying a gift for Father. It's his birthday. His shaving mug is chipped and—"

"I'm sure he'll like this one." He hadn't often seen her this flustered. She looked tired. The rich green of her dress accented the green in her eyes but didn't disguise the circles beneath those eyes. Wasn't she sleeping well?

"Mrs. Johansen, who used to be our cook, is baking a cake.

With all my practice my cakes still can't compare to hers. Of course, she has won the blue ribbon at the county fair for her cakes for the last five years running."

"Amy—"

"She's joining us for dinner. That will be nice. We don't invite company as often as we once did."

"Amy—"

She paused in her uncharacteristic chatter. A slight frown creased her brow. "What are you doing in town in the middle of the morning?"

"I came to see Dr. Matt."

Her gaze dropped to his arm.

"Yes, because of my arm." He took a deep breath. "Truth is, they gave me morphine in the hospital."

Her gaze flew to his, and her eyes widened. "Morphine?"

He nodded, trying to appear nonchalant about it. "I've heard tales of what happens to men who keep taking morphine. I refused it as soon as I could bear the pain without it, though some of the doctors recommended I continue it. I'm out of the strong pain powders I finally talked them into giving me instead. I'm hoping Dr. Matt can give me something."

"I hope so, too."

"Amy, how fortunate I ran into you." Pearl walked up to them briskly, her yellow-and-white dress a spot of cheer in the dark shop. "Do you still want to learn how to refresh the collar and cuffs on your dresses?"

"Yes, but I realize you haven't time to teach me now."

"Things are still busy at the farm. They will be for months. I have enough time to help you, though."

"That would be wonderful. I probably need to buy some material and lace."

"We could look together while Frank is busy here. I have some items to pick up at the general store anyway." She lifted her brows in friendly question. "You don't mind meeting us there when you're done with Father, do you, Frank?"

"Of course not."

A creak notified Frank the doctor's office door was opening. A glance over his shoulder verified it. Gray-haired Dr. Matt stood in the doorway and smiled at an equally gray-haired woman while patting her hand in a reassuring manner.

"I'd better grab him before someone else does."

Pearl grinned and shook her head. "I want to say hello to Father first. I promise to only take a moment." She hurried toward the doctor.

"Rather nice to have a doctor in the family, isn't it?" Amy smiled at Frank. "He gives everyone the best of his services, of course, but I imagine even good-hearted doctors have a special place in their hearts for family."

"Hard to imagine what Pearl's life would have been like if Dr. Matt and his wife hadn't taken her and her brother into their home when their father left." Frank shook his head. "I never understood how any man could leave a two-year-old daughter and a five-year-old son, just walk away and never come back."

"It seems especially cruel that he left right after their mother died. You'd never suspect that Pearl's life started that way. She has such a positive outlook on life."

A glimmer of hope slid into Frank's heart. If Pearl could heal from such wounds, surely it was possible for God to heal him, too. Frank pulled his thoughts back to the present. "Wish your father a happy birthday for me," he said to Amy.

He wished he were celebrating it with them. Then again, he thought as he crossed to the office, her father would probably rather strike him down than share a meal with him. Not many fathers merrily welcomed men who walked out on their daughters.

Slim was seated on the oak bench when Frank left Dr. Matt's office a few minutes later. The old veteran stood up with a stiff, jerky movement, but if his joints hurt, his face didn't reveal it. A smile shone from a myriad of wrinkles.

"Young Sterling, as I live and breathe. If you ain't a sight for sore eyes, I don't know what is." He reached out with his right hand to shake Frank's, realized his error, and held out his left instead.

Frank put his hat on his head to free his hand to shake with Slim. "Good to see you."

Dr. Matt leaned against the doorpost. "You here to see me, Slim?"

"Sure am, Doc. Like to take a minute to talk with our hero here first, if you don't mind."

Doc nodded. "You know where to find me." He entered his office and left the two veterans alone.

A quick glance about the store assured Frank that Pearl and Amy had left. He had time to talk. "Appreciate the sentiment, Slim, but I'm hardly a hero."

Slim's smile disappeared. "I know what war is like. Every soldier is a hero. Either that or a fool or both."

Frank chuckled. "Both, I think."

"Probably so. Saw you talking to that pretty young lady of yours earlier. Yes, sir, you're a lucky man coming home to her."

"She's a fine woman, that's certain, but she's no longer mine."

"Throw you over when you came home with that arm?" He didn't wait for an answer. "Well, good riddance to her, I say. Women are all alike beneath those soft, sweet faces. My girl did the same to me when I came home from the war with this." He slapped his palm against the thigh above the wooden leg. "Said she wanted a whole man. Said she knew I'd understand."

Frank's stomach turned over. "I'm sorry." It was the first he'd heard of this woman. How had Slim endured her betrayal? If Amy had acted that way. . . "You never married?"

"Met a couple ladies I considered courting. In the end, I just couldn't trust them." He leaned closer and said in a loud whisper. "I don't tell that to just anyone, you know."

"I'll keep your confidence."

"Sorry about Miss Henderson. I thought she was the type to stick by a man no matter what."

It seemed cruel to correct Slim's misconception that Frank was a fellow victim of a betraying woman, but to allow it to stand was unfair to Amy. The way gossip flew around this town, if he didn't straighten out the facts, everyone would be prattling off the wrong story by lamp-lighting time.

Frank cleared his throat. "You're right about Amy. She isn't the type of woman to walk away from a man because he loses an arm. I don't want people thinking she is. I'm the one who walked away."

"You have a woman like that and you walk away?" Slim crossed his arms over his chest and shook his head.

"Excuse me." A plump woman in her forties stopped beside them. "Are you two waiting to see the doctor?"

"Doc's waiting on me," Slim informed her. "Best get in there." He nodded at Frank. "Glad you got back, even if you aren't all in one piece. And I'm not talking about your arm." He pointed at his head and chuckled as he stepped toward the office door.

Frank didn't join in the chuckle. Thoughts of the woman who betrayed Slim clung to him as he went about his day. Thank the Lord, Amy hadn't been repulsed by him. Adjusting to a future without her was difficult enough under the present circumstances. He could only imagine the depth of the pain if that bleak future was the result of Amy's revulsion.

Maybe Slim was right. Maybe he was a fool to walk away from Amy. But his love for her meant he wanted life's best for her.

His boots clunked against the boardwalk as he walked toward the general store. *Please give her a beautiful life, Lord. And if it's not too late after all these years, please heal Slim's heart.*

His own heart clenched. *Will I end up bitter like Slim because I walked away from Amy's love?*

# nine

"Hello, Amy." Pearl looked across the kitchen from where she stirred a large pot with a wooden spoon. Little Viola perched on one of her mother's hips and stared diligently into the pot. "I saw Maggie helping you with your buggie and horse, or I would have gone out to help you."

Maggie patted Amy's arm. "She's getting good at unhitching."

Amy set her basket on the kitchen table. "I think you're flattering me. I do believe I'm getting better at it, but I'm still not comfortable doing it myself. I'm afraid I'll undo something in the wrong order and mess myself up."

She crossed the room and held out her arms. "Hello, Viola. May I hold you today?"

Viola shifted her wide-eyed gaze from the bubbling pot to Amy, considered the offer in silence, then with a sudden move leaned toward Amy. The women laughed as Amy drew the girl into her arms. "You are the sweetest thing." Amy dropped a kiss onto Viola's forehead.

"She's been a rascal today," Pearl confided. "Every time I turned my back for even the briefest moment, she'd find something dangerous."

"The beetle wasn't dangerous," Maggie protested with a grin. "Just untasty."

Amy wrinkled her nose. "Ish."

Pearl nodded. "Exactly."

"This looks much better than beetles." Amy glanced at the golden mixture bubbling on the stove. "Mmm. Applesauce."

"Mmm." Viola pressed her lips together and moved them back and forth. "Mmm."

The women laughed, delighted by the girl's simple imitation.

Pearl lifted her eyebrows and smiled at the girl. "Where is Amy?"

Viola frowned slightly, then pushed a pudgy finger into Amy's cheek.

"That's right," Pearl praised. "Can you say Amy?"

Viola's finger went into her mouth. "Mmm."

Maggie brushed her hand across Viola's curls. "Don't feel bad. She can't say Maggie yet, either, and I work on it every day with her."

"Uh. Uh." The little girl wiggled in Amy's arms.

Amy laughed. "She gets her ideas across pretty well without words. I think she wants to get down, but I don't dare put her down here so close to the hot stove."

Maggie reached for Viola. "I'll take her outside."

Amy's heart felt the emptiness when Viola settled into Maggie's arms. She'd so often dreamed of raising children with Frank. Now that dream appeared dead, along with so many others.

"I do worry about this winter," Pearl confided as the screen door banged closed behind Maggie. "Now that Viola's learned to walk, she usually runs instead. Even with all of us watching, she's almost too quick for us sometimes. Can't let our guard down for a minute. This winter the stove will be heated almost all the time and the parlor stove, too. I told Jason we should fence them off. I was only partly in jest."

"I'm sure you will all watch over her and keep her safe."

Pearl sighed. "We try."

"Where are Grace and Chalmers?"

"I sent them outside to play. Chalmers has been into trouble all day today, just like his little sister. He was determined to help Andy carry out the pail of stove ashes this morning. Of course, he tripped on the porch steps."

"Did he hurt himself?"

"No, but he was gray from head to toe."

Amy smiled. "You're very fortunate, you know, to have this wonderful family."

A sweet smile grew slowly across Pearl's face. "Yes, I do know."

"I wasn't sure whether I should come out today."

"Why? I expected you. You aren't in the least in the way."

"I don't think Frank would agree. Is. . .is he home?"

"He's outside somewhere. Probably in the barn. I never saw a man or child who loves animals the way Frank does." Pearl pulled the iron pot to a covered burner. "This can cool now. Let's move the table and a couple chairs over by the window. We'll be able to see our stitches better there, and it will be cooler."

Amy settled her chair beside the window, welcoming the breeze, which caused the curtains to wave gently into the room. She glanced up at a sampler on the nearby wall. "I've always loved that sampler. 'Charity hopeth all things.' "

"Frank and Jason's mother made it." Pearl leaned against the back of her chair and looked at the sampler. "I treasure it. It was a great strength to me during the months right after Jason and I married."

"It must have been difficult. You not only married Jason but his family."

"That wasn't the difficult part. At least, it didn't seem difficult. I don't think I've ever told anyone the truth about Jason's proposal."

Amy touched Pearl's arm gently. "You needn't confide anything in me unless you want to."

"I want to." Pearl took a deep breath. "As you know, I loved Jason since we were children. I was ecstatic when he asked me to marry him. But almost as soon as I said yes, he indicated he wanted a wife to help him with his younger brothers and sisters. His parents had died only a few weeks earlier. Then I realized he hadn't said he loved me. He didn't mention love at all before he asked me to marry him or for a long time after the wedding."

Amy stared at Pearl, shocked. "But he is so in love with you. It's in the way he looks at you and moves around you so naturally and, well, just everything about the way he is around you."

A blush brightened Pearl's cheeks. "Now, perhaps, but not back then. I asked the Lord to let Jason love me. And I kept hoping. I read every verse on hope in the Bible I could find. I needed to know more about hope because it was so hard for me to hope for Jason's love." She laid her hand over Amy's. "I'll be hoping for you and Frank, too."

Tears welled up in Amy's eyes. "Thank you." She took a deep breath and lifted the linen towel from its protective position on top of the basket. "We'd best start our work."

Amy pulled the yellow linen gown from the basket. "I probably shouldn't waste the time on this one. Summer is almost over."

"There'll be more hot days yet. This is the gown we bought the lace for, isn't it?"

Pearl explained how Amy could replace the frayed linen cuffs with ruffled lace. Amy gave her full attention. Seated on the oak kitchen chair, she began removing the cuff with care so she didn't tear the sleeve.

Pearl brought a man's brown cotton shirt out, sat down beside Amy, and began removing the shirt collar. "This needs turning," she explained in response to Amy's questioning look. "There's a sheet that needs redoing, too, but I haven't time for that today."

"A sheet?"

"Yes. The middle is quite worn."

"How can you hide that?"

"I can't hide it, but I can make it last longer. I'll tear it down the middle and restitch it back together with the edges in the middle."

"You are a marvel, Pearl Sterling."

"Hardly that."

•

Amy lifted the detached yellow linen cuffs. "There. Now what?"

Pearl showed her how to place the lace, overlapping it at even intervals to form a dainty ruffle, anchoring the lace with pins. The stitch required was simple but tiny.

Amy worked at the table, her concentration wholly given to pinning the lace. When she completed pinning it to one sleeve, she placed her porcelain thimble on her finger and began making careful stitches.

She shook her head, keeping her attention on her work. "I am so ignorant. I never knew people redid their clothes and sheets. I barely know how to sew. Maybe Frank is right not to marry me. Maybe he needs a wife who knows all the things I don't."

"That's only your fear talking. Frank needs a wife who loves him as much as you love him."

Amy managed a shaky smile. "That's what you always say. I'm glad you do."

" 'Charity hopeth all things.' "

"Maybe it would be wiser for me not to hope, but I don't know how. Most of the time I'm certain Frank will come to his senses and realize we are meant to be together. I keep reminding myself that I have to be strong for him. I always knew there's much for me to learn to be the farm wife he needs. But now it's even more important when chores are so much more difficult and time consuming for him. I'll need to take care of the house and garden and chickens. Will you teach me to milk a cow?" She looked up from her stitching.

Pearl laughed. "I'm afraid not. Frank tried to teach me once. Jason was furious. He said he didn't want his wife to smell like cows." She leaned forward, her eyes sparkling, and dropped her voice slightly. "I thought it a rather good reason not to do the milking."

Amy joined her in a chuckle, but she didn't change her mind. Things were different for her and Frank—or they would be when Frank remembered God meant them to spend their lives together. If he remembered.

"Jason is awfully worried about Frank. We all are, but Jason especially. They were so close growing up, though for a time after their parents died, there was a rift between them."

Amy nodded. "Frank told me. He thought Jason was trying to take over their father's place in the family. Frank wanted to go to school to learn more about agriculture, and Jason told him they couldn't afford it."

"Since Jason is the oldest, he naturally felt the responsibility of running the farm and caring for the family fell to him."

"All Frank could see was his world falling apart." Amy understood Pearl's need to defend Jason's behavior, but Amy felt the same need to defend Frank. She was glad their friendship could withstand the truth and that it was always kindly spoken to each other. "Frank always loved farming. It's all he's ever wanted to do. He said Jason never wanted to be a farmer. He wants to be an architect. That's what you told me, too."

"Yes."

"Frank felt Jason was stealing his future."

Pearl's hands stopped in the middle of a stitch. Surprise stood large in her eyes. "I didn't know that. Jason never intended to take the farm away from Frank. He only wanted to keep the farm going to support the family."

"Frank knows that now. He was only eighteen at the time and grieving over the loss of his parents, the same as Jason. Frank said it took a long time for him to understand that Jason felt as though his calling had also been stolen when their parents died. Giving up the profession for which he'd trained must have been a painful sacrifice for Jason."

"It was." Pearl lowered the brown material to her lap. "Those were awful days for everyone." She caught her bottom lip between her teeth.

Amy saw the gleam in her friend's eyes. "I know that look. You've a secret and can't decide whether to share it."

"You always keep my confidences, but this involves other people."

"Then follow your conscience." Amy went back to her stitching.

For a minute, only sounds coming through the window were audible: the breeze rustling the leaves of the lilac bushes near the porch, a cow making an announcement to another cow out in the pasture, bees buzzing busily among the flowers beside the steps.

Amy's thoughts quickly turned from her friend's secret to Frank. He seemed always central in her thoughts. What exactly was he doing now? Did she hover in his thoughts as he hovered in hers?

"Oh, I want to tell you. Jason won't mind." Pearl leaned forward, the cotton shirt a pile in her lap, her eyes sparkling. "Jason is working at his architectural design again."

"Why, that's wonderful. Is he designing something special? Has he sold his designs?"

"Yes and yes. He's designed homes and outbuildings for a few people over the years since we married but not enough to make much money from it. He didn't try to sell his designs himself. First Thor asked him to design their new farmhouse after the fire burned down their old home. The next year another farmer asked him to design a home. People liked his work and recommended him to others. He's designed maybe half a dozen buildings now."

"That's wonderful. Why is this a secret? I'd think he'd want people to know."

"He hasn't the time to put into it to make a living at it. Now he's been asked to submit a design for the new bank and for the bank president's house as well. He's barely slept lately, between that and harvest. He starts after the field work is done and works by lamplight late into the night." Pearl's face softened, and Amy knew her friend was picturing her husband at work. "When he begins designing in the evening, he's exhausted. But it doesn't take long for him to become so involved in his work that he forgets his fatigue." She grinned. "Until morning, that is."

"If he's awarded the contracts for these buildings, maybe it will be the step he needs."

Pearl picked her work back up and shook her head. "I don't think so. Jason wouldn't leave the farm now. He feels Frank needs him here."

"Has he told Frank that?"

"No, he'd never do that. He doesn't want Frank to feel he's a burden."

Sadness gave a heaviness to Amy's chest. "Frank will sense it," she said quietly.

"I hope not."

Amy didn't insist, but she knew in her heart Frank would know his brother was sacrificing for him. She wanted to believe it would make Frank feel loved. She knew instead that he'd feel pitied and hate it.

She changed the subject. "How is Frank's health? He looks tired."

"He is awfully tired, I'm afraid."

Amy didn't like the frown that furrowed Pearl's forehead."He insists on working every day," Pearl continued. " 'I'll carry my own weight,' he says, but he can't do much yet. It takes very little to wear him out. Father warned him to rest more, but Frank won't hear of it. And of course, the pain is difficult for him sometimes."

Remembering that Frank had refused morphine, Amy shuddered. He was in so many kinds of pain, and she was shut out from helping him relieve any of them. Was there anything in life more horrible than knowing you couldn't help someone you love?

They soon set aside their mending to prepare lunch. Pearl encouraged Amy to continue her stitching, but it made Amy uncomfortable when she could be helping Pearl. Soon a roast was braised and placed in the oven. A trip to the garden was a refreshing change from spending the morning indoors. They washed the potatoes and carrots beneath the outside pump, the cold water chilling their hands.

Maggie volunteered to pick fresh corn for lunch. She brought back a basketful. Amy joined Pearl and Maggie on the back porch steps, husking the corn. Amy liked the sweet smell of the large yellow kernels. She liked the silky feel of the tassels. She liked the friendly conversation. She liked working in the sunshine, so different than working alone inside her tiny apartment kitchen.

She did not like the occasional worm she found.

Viola had no such compunctions. The women spent almost as much time keeping Viola from searching for the creatures in the discarded husks as they did husking.

All the time she worked, Amy thought how she'd love to be living this life every day, performing simple homely duties like preparing a meal for Frank, working with his family, feeling one with them. For years she'd believed this would be her future. *I can't believe Frank has chosen that this won't happen for us, Lord. I can't believe he won't come back to us again. I won't believe it.* Time and again she blinked back tears, trying to hide from her friends the pain that never ceased.

*Maybe if I'm around Frank, he will change his mind,* she thought. *Surely seeing me will make it harder for him to forget the love we shared.*

Yet part of her wondered whether keeping hope was wise. Would the pain increase if she allowed herself to hope and Frank didn't change his mind? *He must change his mind,* her thoughts insisted. The verse on the sampler rang through her head. *Charity hopeth all things.* How could hope not be wise when the Bible spoke of it so highly?

At noon while Amy joined Pearl and Maggie in the kitchen with last-minute preparations, her heart picked up its beat.

The mixture of joy and trepidation left her feeling uncharacteristically giddy, though she hoped she appeared calm, happy, and nonchalant.

She heard the three brothers at the basin on the back porch before she saw them. Jason was the first to enter the kitchen. The smells of earth and sweat and kerosene entered with him and mingled with the kitchen odors. Amy had found the smells of the working men unpleasant at first. Now the smells only spoke the happy fact that the men were home from the fields.

"Papa." Delight filled little Chalmers's voice when he spotted Jason entering the kitchen. The boy raced across the room, arms outstretched.

Viola, who'd been happily banging a pot lid against the floor, turned at the word "Papa" and squealed with joy. The pot lid was forgotten as she stood and headed for her father in a run.

Jason swooped Chalmers into his arms. "Hello, Son. Have you been a good boy for Mother?"

"Yes. Have you been good?"

Laughter filled the air.

"I've been working," Jason replied, setting Chalmers down and lifting Viola, who had wrapped her arms around his denim-covered leg.

"I do believe you avoided our son's question," Pearl teased, wiping her hands on her apron. "What could you possibly have been doing out in the fields but behaving yourself?"

Jason dropped a kiss on her cheek. "I'll never tell."

Amy loved watching the little family. Was there anything more wonderful than spending life surrounded by those you loved?

She knew the moment Frank entered the room. She glanced up from the bread plate she was filling to smile at him.

His brown eyes were stormy.

He didn't greet her. The slight dampened the giddy feeling, but Amy continued to smile. She didn't want anyone to see how strongly his anger shook her. Why was he so unfriendly? He hadn't acted that way at the store last week.

*At least I'm not seated next to him or directly across from him,* she thought as she took her seat following grace. Frank sat on the other side of the table but at the other end.

Filling plates from the overflowing platters and bowls kept everyone's attention for a few minutes. Jason and Andy quickly assured Pearl that the meal "hit the spot."

Amy glanced at Frank while accepting a bowl of cucumbers and onions in vinegar from Pearl, who sat beside her. Frank's tan showed the time he'd spent in the fields since arriving home, though his face didn't show the typical farmer's hat line yet.

He squinted in a frown and rolled the shoulder of his wounded arm.

The movement tightened her throat.

Was he in pain? Was the medicine Dr. Matt gave him sufficiently strong to fight the discomfort? Likely Frank was also battling the normal aches that anyone would feel upon entering back into life after months in a hospital. A little sigh escaped her at the thought of how much he faced.

Frank looked up and their gazes met. She chanced a small smile.

He didn't return it. He turned his attention to his meal.

Amy took a bite of potatoes, but she'd lost her appetite.

A couple bites later she realized the usually talkative family was quiet. It only made her more uneasy believing she and Frank were causing discomfort for the others. Even Viola and Chalmers weren't chattering.

"Frank's had some news about his division," Jason finally announced.

Everyone looked at Frank.

He laid down his fork. "The Thirteenth is coming home. They embarked August thirteenth."

Andy shifted in his chair. "Does that mean they're through fighting?"

Frank nodded. "It will probably be awhile before they're mustered out. They'll land in San Francisco. I suppose they'll travel to Fort Snelling in St. Paul after that."

"Maybe you'll see some of the men when they get back," Jason suggested.

"Not likely. None of them are from around here." Frank still hadn't cracked a smile.

"What about that man you've received letters from?" Pearl asked. "I think you said his name is Dan."

"Dan Terrell. He's from the other side of the state. Not much chance we'll see each other."

Amy remembered Frank mentioning Dan's name often in his letters. "Mr. Terrell is from the Northfield area, isn't he?"

"Yes." The quick glance Frank gave her wasn't friendly. She felt as though it was a warning to keep silent. Did he not even want such a simple reminder that he'd once shared his life with her?

Silence fell on the group again. Amy was aware the family darted looks from her to Frank and back. She hated their discomfort and her own. Why did Frank insist on acting as though the two of them were feuding?

Frank cleared his throat. "There are farms in the Philippines; at least there were farms there before we arrived. Our camp was in a peanut field."

No one said anything, but they gave Frank their full attention.

"Not a day went by but I thought about that poor farmer. Land he'd toiled over, his livelihood, his support for his family—and we slept and ate on it." He looked up, and his gaze moved from one to another around the table. "What if that were our farm? What if an army camped in our fields? What if armies shot at each other around our buildings and animals?"

The quiet, almost emotionless tone added to the chill his words sent through Amy.

Frank's gaze shifted to Chalmers, who chewed on a piece of buttered bread. "What if armies were in our fields shooting at each other around Chalmers and Viola?"

Everyone was still. They'd all stopped eating. The horror Frank presented made Amy feel sick to her stomach. She suspected the others' reactions were similar.

"The farmer will be able to clean up his field now." Frank lifted his fork. "Quite a chore, I imagine."

Jason cleared his throat. "Yes, I should think so."

No one spoke after that. Amy's thoughts whirled around Frank's war experience. How many awful things were trapped inside his mind? Her heart ached for him.

Amy didn't finish her meal, nor did Maggie, though the others managed to do so. The pie Pearl had baked that morning wasn't touched. No one had the stomach for dessert.

After the men left, the girls began clearing the table. "Why don't we sit on the porch and rest for a few minutes while the girls wash up the dishes, Amy?" Pearl led the way, carrying Viola propped on her hip.

Amy's composure had outwardly held together during the meal, but now that she was alone with Pearl, it broke. She pulled a lace-trimmed hanky from her apron pocket and caught the tears that spilled onto her cheeks. "I never thought Frank would ignore me like that, especially in front of other people."

"I didn't either." Unease threaded through Pearl's quiet reply.

"I suppose he thinks by coming out here I'm trying to push my way back into his life. He's using his silence to yell at me that my attempt is not going to work." Amy hugged herself, as though by doing so she could force her pain to leave.

Pearl shifted Viola from one hip to the other. "You're my friend. You're a friend to all of us. You're always welcome here."

"Thank you."

"Oh!" Viola reached out a pudgy hand, her fingers opening and closing. Amy followed the child's wide-eyed gaze. Viola's fascination was caught by a Monarch butterfly, which flew over the pansies beside the porch with grace. The child squirmed in her mother's arms, anxious to get down and run after the butterfly.

Pearl laughed. "Oh, no you don't, Viola. You'll never catch the butterfly, no matter how hard you try, but you'll trample my flowers in the attempt."

The picture brought a small smile to Amy, but it also tugged at her heart. "Do you know how blessed you are?" The tears clogging her throat caused the words to waver.

Pearl's gaze met hers. She nodded. "Yes, I do. Which makes seeing Frank trying to push away his love for you and seeing how painful that is for both of you all the harder to watch. I'm so sorry, Amy. I wish there was something I could do."

Amy gave a strangled little laugh. "So do I. I'd better leave. I shouldn't have come in the first place."

"Frank will come to his senses eventually."

Amy remembered Pearl's statement half an hour later as she turned the horse and buggy from the farm drive onto the narrow road. She had to believe Frank would come to his senses. She had to keep hoping. *If I don't, how can I bear to face the future, Lord?*

Frank's treatment of her at lunch rolled back into her mind. How could he treat her that way? Her face grew hot at the memory. Anger surged in a wave from the embarrassment. Her back straightened. The muscles in her face tightened. "How dare he?" She flicked the reins to hurry the horse to a pace more in keeping with her anger. "There's no reason for him to act so. . .so. . .childishly. He could act civil toward me."

She nursed the anger along, feeding it excuses and painful memories the way she fed kindling to a fire. The anger relieved the pain somewhat.

"How dare he try to make me feel I'm wrong to visit Pearl?"

Guilt wiggled into her thoughts. She'd known, hoped, she might see Frank when she visited Pearl for help with her mending. Of course, he knew that, too. How could he not?

The anger unraveled a bit back into pain. She immediately

threw in another piece of mental kindling. The reason for her visit didn't justify his refusal to act like a gentleman. There was no need for him to purposely build thick walls between them. Did he think she was going to storm those walls, to force a confrontation, to force him to admit he loved her?

Truth weakened her defenses. She would storm those walls if she knew how. She would attack his defenses if she believed doing so would force him to admit his love.

Clarity struck so swiftly that she pulled the horse up short. It neighed in protest.

Frank knew what he was doing in building the walls. He wanted to feed his own anger. What better way to protect himself?

Wasn't she welcoming anger to protect herself from the pain of losing his love?

"You wouldn't choose anger to avoid pain, dear Jesus. I won't choose it, either. But this is a new path for me, Lord. Show me how to love him the way You love him, without anger and without insisting he return my love."

The desire to tell Frank what she thought of his behavior still whispered in her thoughts. She struggled to put those temptations away. "What would You say to him in my place, Lord?"

The thought came swift and sure. *My wish for him is the same as for all My children. I wish him love and peace and healing.*

Amy took a deep breath and closed her eyes. "Dear Lord, please bring love and peace and healing into Frank's life. Amen."

She opened her eyes, flicked the reins, and urged the horse to start. Queen Anne's lace, purple thistle, and daisies danced in the wild grass along the roadside. She hadn't noticed them earlier; she'd seen only her anger and pain.

Enduring her own pain wasn't nearly as searing as feeling his.

# ten

Summer slid into colorful, pungent autumn. The green of leaves, grass, and fields muted into golden and brown relieved by splashes of burgundy. Corn harvest filled farmers' days. Huskings and harvest dances livened the evenings. V's of geese patterned the sky at dawn and dusk. The full orange harvest moon commanded the night.

Amy stayed away from the farm. She threw her energy into preparing for the fall classes at Windom Academy. When she wasn't working on class preparation, she spent all the hours she dared spare painting. Attempts to capture the glories of autumn demanded concentration. She welcomed the respite, however brief, from thoughts of Frank.

For the first time in her life, she dreaded attending church. It meant seeing Frank. Sometimes he honored her with a solemn nod of recognition. More often he ignored her, talking with other people and avoiding so much as a glance in her direction. She was certain he was as aware of her presence as she was of his. The pain twisted her insides and made concentration on the worship impossible. She left every service with a prayer asking God's forgiveness for her inattention.

"I'd spend the morning with my thoughts more on the Lord if Frank weren't there," Amy grumbled to Pearl.

Fall term at the academy didn't bring the relief for which she hoped. A friendly camaraderie existed between most students and the small faculty. The returning students' questions and her reply became a refrain: "Yes, Frank did return from the war. Thank you for asking after him. He's wounded but alive. We've cancelled our plans to marry." The inevitable expression of sympathy followed. "Thank you." Then the smile and attempt to redirect the conversation. "What about you? How was your summer?"

A number of male students from the academy had joined the service after war was declared. None of them made it to the battlefields. Amy knew she was more deeply grateful for that fact than were the young men who'd so eagerly offered themselves. Now some of the women came up with an idea that rapidly gained favor: a celebration honoring all the young men in the area who had joined the service because of the war.

"The pictures of the soldier leaving for and returning from war will be perfect for the celebration," Mrs. Headley told Amy. "We'll hang them in a conspicuous place at the reception."

"Oh, no, please." Amy sought frantically for an excuse, any excuse but the true one. "The print of the soldier leaving is so well known. People will think it presumptuous if my painting of the returning soldier is shown beside it."

The headmaster's wife patted Amy's hand. "My dear, the townspeople will think it most appropriate, I assure you. The people are as proud of your talent as if it were their own."

Amy smiled weakly. She considered Mrs. Headley a friend, but even to her she didn't want to admit her fear.

Everyone in town knew she'd expected to welcome Frank home to her arms like the woman in her painting welcomed home the soldier. Everyone knew Frank broke their engagement. People might not speak to her face of the similarity of the painting to her expectations, but she was certain they'd be thinking of it.

For Amy, the celebration was only another expectation of pain at seeing the man she loved. She helped prepare for it with a heavy heart.

❧

*I feel like a stranger here,* Frank thought, looking at the crowd in the academy hall.

Men in military uniforms filled the rectangular room. He'd lived among military men for over a year. *Why don't they seem familiar?*

Dan Terrell, who Frank had unexpectedly met in St. Paul just a week before, leaned close. "The man who spoke at the presentation earlier said none of these men fought in the war, right?"

"Right. It seems the entire group got no farther than one of the stateside camps."

"Battled typhoid fever but not the Spanish or Filipinos."

"That's the way I understand it." Frank smiled. "So that's it."

Dan raised his eyebrows in question. "What is?"

"That's why I feel like a stranger among these men, even though they were in the military and I've known most of them all my life."

"I think after a man's fought in a war, he's a stranger for the rest of his life to everyone who hasn't fought in one." The words were spoken matter-of-factly.

Frank looked at his friend. Dan met his gaze steadily.

This was one of the reasons he treasured Dan's friendship, Frank realized. They spoke the truth to each other, the truth they often wouldn't admit to others. They spoke it straight out, without waxing maudlin about it.

Dan indicated a table across the room. "Those refreshments look mighty tempting. What say we check them out? My stomach is growling."

"That's Amy at the right end of the table, the one serving punch."

"So that's why we're standing over here starving. You're avoiding her."

Frank and Amy's friend, Sylvia, and Mrs. Headley stopped to welcome them, relieving Frank of the necessity of replying to his friend's all-too-accurate observation.

Frank had always thought of Sylvia as rather the silly sort, though good-hearted. Now she wore a sober air. He knew instinctively that she was thinking of Roland, wishing he were here, remembering he would never be with her again in this lifetime.

Frank took hold of one of her hands. "I'm sorry for your loss. Roland confided in me how much he cared for you. I couldn't believe it when Amy wrote me that Roland died from the typhoid. I'll miss him. We had a lot of good times together."

Her eyes misted over. "Thank you."

"Do you remember that night years ago when a group of us walked home from a Christmas party together?"

She nodded. "The party was held in this very room."

He'd forgotten that. "Amy slipped on the walking bridge that spans the ravine."

"And her hat went tumbling into the gorge below." She laughed.

"That's right. The next day I searched for it. It took me hours, but I finally located it up in a tall bush. I took it over to Amy's house to return it. In front of her house, who do I run into but Roland. He spots the hat and starts teasing me about it. That was before Amy and I started courting. I was one embarrassed fellow, I can tell you."

She gave his hand a squeeze and smiled. "Thank you for sharing such a fun memory."

Sylvia and Mrs. Headley moved on.

"Brave enough to face Amy yet?" Dan asked. "Or will I be obliged to bring you punch and a piece of one of those incredible looking cakes?"

Frank shot him a dirty look and headed across the room. Well-wishers stopped them every few steps. "You've met nearly the entire town," Frank told Dan as they reached the refreshment table.

"Not this lady." Dan smiled at Amy. "Aren't you going to introduce us?"

Amy blushed.

Beneath the calm, polite exterior Frank struggled to maintain, he seethed. He'd ignored Amy for two months. Dan knew he'd broken up with her. Why was he insisting on putting them in this position? "Dan, this is Miss Amy Henderson. Miss Henderson, this is Mr. Dan Terrell. We—"

"Mr. Terrell, I'm delighted to meet you." Amy beamed at Dan. "Frank wrote me about you."

"I hope he said as many nice things about me as he told me about you."

Frank caught the pleased look Amy darted at him. He felt his face heat. "Dan—"

"Miss Henderson, we are about to faint from hunger and thirst. May we sample some of that spicy smelling punch you're dishing out?"

She laughed, filled a crystal cup with the golden liquid, and handed it to him. "Would you like a cup, too, Frank?"

He nodded.

Dan pointed to two pictures on the wall above the table. "Those are certainly appropriate. I've seen copies of the one with the soldier leaving before, but the one of the soldier returning looks like an original oil painting."

"It is," Amy admitted.

Frank studied the picture of the returning soldier. The man and woman in the painting looked as though they could walk right off the canvas they were so alive. Their love for each other and joy in their reunion shone from their faces, from every line of their bodies. Frank knew in an instant that Amy had painted the picture from her heart, knew that he was the man in the picture and the woman was Amy, though the faces in the painting weren't theirs.

"You painted this." He continued staring at the picture as he spoke to her.

"Yes."

He couldn't take his eyes off the picture. His heart drank in the love she'd expressed for him in it. She'd laid her own heart open for the world to see how much she loved him and how deeply she longed for him to return from the war to her. He knew he shouldn't allow himself to welcome this. If he let down the barriers he'd put up against her, it would be difficult rebuilding them. But he was so tired of all the battling with life he'd done the last couple months, of all the battles he envisioned before him in the years to come, that he yearned for a respite, even if only for a moment.

"When did you paint this?" he asked when he could speak again.

"Soon after you were sent to the Philippines."

"You didn't tell me."

"No. Paintings are hard to express in words."

"Frank told me you painted, Miss Henderson, but I had no idea the extent of your talent."

"Thank you, Mr. Terrell."

"Did you paint the picture hanging in the Sterlings' parlor—the one of Pearl's parents?" Dan asked.

"Yes, I did. It was Jason's gift to Pearl for their first Christmas. I painted it from an old photograph of the couple on their wedding day. Pearl lost her parents when she was only two, so the picture meant a great deal to her."

Dan's brown eyes seemed to light up. "I wonder if you'd be so kind as to paint a portrait of my wife and I on our wedding day from a photograph, like you did Pearl's parents."

"I'll be glad to paint it for you. Is it a gift for your wife?"

Dan set his cup on the table. "I'm a widower, Miss Henderson."

She touched the back of his hand in a quick, spontaneous gesture. "I'm so sorry. I'll begin the painting as soon as possible. I teach art here at the academy, so you can send the photograph to me here. How will I deliver the painting to you? You live near Northfield, I understand."

"Not anymore. I'm a resident of this county now."

Frank decided it was time to explain. "Dan and I ran into each other in St. Paul last week."

"At the parade?"

"Yes." President McKinley had traveled to St. Paul to personally review the Thirteenth in its final march before mustering out. Frank had been surprised at the pride he'd felt marching before the country's most important man. It had been both joyful and painful to see the men he'd fought beside. Strange that only among them did he feel completely comfortable without his arm.

The only time he'd felt uncomfortable that day was when he'd been presented a medal for bravery. What was brave about doing what you had to in a life or death situation, he'd wondered.

He'd thought about Amy so many times during the parade day. Had she attended? If so, she hadn't attended with his family. He'd purposely refrained from asking Pearl. He didn't want to admit he still cared.

He hoped Amy had seen the parade.

He shifted his thoughts with an effort. "Dan's agreed to stay at the farm through the winter."

Dan grinned. "That's a nice way of saying I'm the latest hired help."

"He's a good farmer. We need someone like him around the farm."

"You've never seen me working as a farmhand," Dan reminded him in a wry tone.

"I've seen you under fire. I know the kind of man you are." At Dan's embarrassment, Frank changed the subject. "I'm ready to head back to the farm if you are, Dan. Much more of this celebrate-the-returning-hero stuff, and our heads will be too large to fit through the barn door come morning."

It was with reluctance that Frank said good night to Amy.

He was fiercely glad for the excuse Dan had given him to ignore the walls he'd so carefully and firmly built up since arriving home. Still, he had every intention of putting those walls back in place immediately.

After all, the soldier Amy painted had returned with both arms intact.

❧

A few weeks later, Amy stood in the academy art studio, surveying the canvas on an easel with a critical eye. She'd completed the painting days ago and hadn't looked at it since. She'd wanted to distance herself from it in order to view it with a semblance of objectivity.

Did her figures look as much like Dan Terrell and his wife in their wedding picture as possible? Did they look as lifelike as her abilities allowed? Would a little more shadow beneath his bride's chin help, or had she caught the lighting correctly?

Finally she gave a satisfied nod. "Yes, it is as good as I thought."

The afternoon was crisp and clear. She had no more classes scheduled. Even though it was only two days before Thanksgiving, no snow or ice had turned the roads into threatening passages. She would deliver it to Mr. Terrell that afternoon.

Amy pushed back her eagerness at the possibility of seeing Frank and concentrated on packing the painting with care. The painting was dry enough to deliver with only limited danger of damage.

The fields were either black after their turning by the plow or stubbly. Amy knew that to some people the November landscape seemed barren compared to the lush August fields she'd passed the last time she'd visited the farm. The artist in her saw beauty in patterns and shadows in the late fall fields.

As she entered the farmyard, her gaze searched for Frank. He wasn't in sight.

He'd acted curt toward her at the reception honoring the

veterans last month, but at least he'd spoken to her. Since then when they'd run into each other at church each Sunday, he'd said hello and smiled. He'd taken part in conversations she'd had with Pearl and Jason. Twice he'd shared a laughing glance with her when a comment by Jason elicited a common memory. Surely God must be healing Frank's wounds.

The process seemed agonizingly slow to her, but at least her hope that Frank would return to them appeared possible and not a silly flight of fancy.

Amy was tying the horse to the hitching rail when Andy came out the back door. "Need some help unhitching your buggy, Miss Amy?"

"No, thank you. I don't expect to be here long enough to unhitch. I've come to deliver a painting to Mr. Terrell. Is he home?"

"He and Frank are in the barn, sharpening tools. I'll fetch him for you."

Pearl held the door for Amy as she carried the painting into the house. The kitchen was warm and inviting after the chill outside air. Sunshine brightened the large room. The pleasant aroma of coffee from the huge enameled pot on the stove welcomed them.

The large oak table stood near the stove. Maggie, grasping the wooden handle of the sad iron, bent over the work shirt on the ironing board, which rested on the table and a nearby kitchen chair. At the other end of the table, Jason studied architectural drawings. Grace sat on the floor, pointing out pictures in a catalog to Viola and Chalmers. Amy suspected it was Grace's responsibility to keep the little ones away from the hot stove and irons.

Amy laid the painting on the table. A moment later, Dan entered the house. Disappointment slipped past Amy's defenses when she saw Frank wasn't with him.

Excitement filled Dan's slender face. "Andy said you

brought my painting, Miss Henderson. I didn't expect it for another month at least."

Dan drew off his gloves and began cautiously removing the protective cloth. The family gathered around to watch.

At a cold rush of air, Amy looked over her shoulder toward the kitchen door to see Frank enter the room. His gaze met hers, and the friendly welcome she saw warmed her heart.

Amy turned her attention back to Dan. Frank stepped up beside her, and the awareness of his presence tingled along her nerves.

When the painting was completely uncovered, Dan and his young bride looked out at the assembled group from the canvas. Compliments for the work poured out.

"It's wonderful, Amy."

"Beautiful."

Dan said nothing.

Was he disappointed? Amy dared a glance at his face. Tears welled in his eyes.

She looked back at the painting. The bride and groom stood beside each other. The bride's large brown eyes beneath thick brows looked confidently toward the future she expected to share with Dan. "Your wife was beautiful."

"Yes." The word was a husky whisper. "Yes, she was beautiful; beautiful through and through." He cleared his throat and tried to continue. He cleared his throat again. "The photograph can't compare to this, Miss Henderson. You've put color and life and warmth into it. It's almost. . .almost like seeing her standing before me again." A tear slid down his cheek. He didn't bother to brush it away.

The intensity of his love and longing for his wife twisted Amy's heart. She suspected the others in the room felt it also, for all fell silent. Frank squeezed her shoulder, and she knew that he, too, felt the sense of reverence for this couple whose life together had been too brief.

"I'll take it to my room now." Dan picked the painting up and turned to Amy. "I'll pay you our agreed-upon price, of course, but no amount of money can pay for what you've given me. Thank you."

No one else in the room moved until Dan entered the stairwell and closed the door behind him. Then throats cleared and people went back to what they'd been about before Dan entered. They walked quickly, moved items noisily, and spoke brightly as if they felt a desperate need to break the spell of Dan's lost love.

"It's your best work yet, Amy." Frank's voice was low and a bit rough with emotion.

Before she could thank him, he started toward the parlor. The small bit of kindness and warmth he'd shown her left her feeling hugged. Was this a sign he was reconsidering his decision about them?

"You'll stay for coffee, won't you?" Pearl asked. "Maggie made apple and cranberry pies this morning. The coffee will warm you for the ride back."

"That's a tempting argument." Not nearly as tempting as spending more time near Frank.

"I'll get your foot warmer." Andy headed for the door. "Might as well heat it up while you're eating."

"Should I unhitch the horse?"

"It'll be all right," Andy assured. "You don't expect to be here more than an hour, do you?"

She assured him she didn't. She hung her coat and muffler on the wooden pegs beside the door, then reached to remove the pins from her hat. "Can I help with anything?"

"Oh, no. Make yourself to home." Pearl entered the pantry. A moment later she returned with a pie. "Maggie, set the ironing board aside so there's room at the table for everyone. I'd invite you into the parlor, Amy, but the stove isn't lit in there. Our teeth would chatter so they'd threaten to break the cups."

In spite of Pearl's insistence that Amy needn't help, she gathered cups from the open shelves and brought them to the table. Then Amy, with an easy familiarity in her friend's kitchen, located the sugar and cream and began pouring coffee. Pearl sliced pie, and Maggie set out a plate of cheese. Andy brought in the metal foot warmer and set it on the stove, then at Pearl's request went to ask Dan to join them for coffee. In the midst of it all, Jason continued to work over his sketches.

Frank entered the room with a copy of *Farm, Stock, and Home* and sat across from Jason. As usual, Frank's presence made all Amy's senses stand up at attention.

Andy returned looking solemn. "Dan says he'll be down in a few minutes, that we should start without him."

The family all took seats at the table. Chalmers climbed up on Frank's lap. The boy pointed to a picture in the magazine. "What's that?"

"It's Uncle Sam, lassoing the Philippines."

Chalmers frowned, obviously not understanding the cartoon. "I don't know Uncle Sam."

The family chuckled.

"I guess you don't at that," Frank replied with a twinkle in his eyes.

The spark caught at Amy's heartstrings. This was the most relaxed and happy she'd seen him since he returned home. Chalmers's blond curls brushed against Frank's brown flannel shirt. The boy appeared completely trusting of Frank and not at all put off by Frank's wounded arm.

Pearl touched Jason's shoulder. "Won't you put away your work for a few minutes and visit with us?"

He grinned sheepishly and stacked the papers in a pile on the end of the table. "Sorry. When I'm working on plans, I tend to get so involved, I forget the world around me."

"I do the same when I paint," Amy told him.

Chalmers slipped down from Frank's lap and took the

magazine with him. "I want to show Dad."

Frank agreed, but Amy thought he looked slightly disappointed as the boy left.

Frank didn't invite Amy to sit beside him, and she hadn't the courage to do so uninvited. Instead she sat at the other end of the table where she could easily see him.

She lifted Viola onto her lap. "Will you sit with me?" The little girl stuck a fingertip in her mouth and studied Amy for a moment, then grinned and rubbed her forehead against Amy's shoulder. Amy rested her head against Viola's for a moment, amazed as always at the softness of Viola's curls.

Amy looked up and caught Frank's gaze on them. She blinked at the hunger in it. In the next moment the hunger was gone as completely as though she'd imagined it. *Had I?* Amy wondered. *Do I only want to believe he longs for us to have a family of our own as much as I do?*

When Frank cut into his piece of pie, Amy noticed how red and chapped his fingers looked.

"How did Dan's wife die, Frank?" Pearl asked.

Frank told them what Dan had shared with him while they were in the Philippines. "He still misses her a great deal, as you saw."

Heavy footsteps on the stairs prevented more questions. Dan joined them at the table with an apology for his tardiness. His red-rimmed eyes made Amy wish there were something she could say or do to comfort him.

"Dan and I started a list of tools we'll need to replace," Frank told Jason. He named a few. He could as well have spoken in another language for all the names meant to Amy.

Pearl smiled across the table at her. "Would you and your father join us for Thanksgiving? We'd love to have you."

"Thank you, but Mrs. Jacobson is already planning our little repast. It would disappoint her terribly if Father and I changed our minds." Would Frank regret her absence? Had he requested that Pearl invite them?

Out of the corner of her eye, she saw Frank move his wounded arm as though to reach for something. He bumped the plate into his coffee cup. Milky brown liquid poured across the table onto Jason's papers.

Frank and Jason leaped to their feet in the same moment. Frank grabbed the cup and righted it.

Jason whipped the papers from the table. He shook coffee from them, splattering it across the linoleum. "Why don't you watch what you're doing?"

"It was an accident." Frank's face was redder than Amy'd ever seen it. "Besides, the table's no place for your work, not when people are eating."

"That's no excuse for clumsiness." Jason took the towel Pearl handed him and dabbed at the papers.

"I suppose you could do better with one arm?"

The heat in Frank's cold tone sent fear through Amy. She fought the desire to reach out to him with a restraining touch. It would likely only increase his anger.

Viola's fingers closed around Amy's collar. Fear filled the child's eyes as she stared at the men. A moment later she burst into sobs. Amy hugged her close, whispering shushing sounds against her hair and rocking.

Chalmers followed Viola's example with a wale.

"Stop arguing this minute." Pearl wiped up the spilled coffee from the table. "You're upsetting the children."

"This is a farm." Frank ignored Pearl's demand and continued his tirade in a louder voice. "You're wasting time designing buildings for other people when there's plenty of work inside our own buildings and outside that needs doing. Andy and Dan and I bust our britches keeping things going while you sit inside and play with those papers."

"*Those papers*, as you call them, bring in money the same as the crops."

Frank slammed his fist on the table and leaned across it, glaring at Jason. "I'd like to see you draw those sketches if you lost your drawing hand."

Maggie gasped.

Everyone stared at Frank.

*You've gone too far. Stop before you say anything worse,* Amy pleaded silently.

"Frank, calm down." Andy scowled at him. "It was an accident, like you said. No call to get in a huff."

"And you." Frank swung toward his younger brother. "You begged to join the service before I left. Bet you're glad now that Jason didn't allow it. Haven't heard you say you wish you'd fought in the war, not since I came back like this." He raised his wounded arm.

A flush spread up Andy's neck and covered his face.

"Frank." Dan's calm voice urged Frank with one word to stop and think.

Jason dropped the papers onto the table. "You came home after the war insisting you could pull your own weight around here. When I said to take it easy, you accused me of pitying you. You know, little brother, there isn't anyone who comes close to pitying you as much as you pity yourself."

"And you don't feel sorry for yourself?" Frank gave a sharp laugh. "You've always resented sacrificing your dreams of becoming an architect for the farm. You didn't think I could run this place even when I had both hands. You had to play the family martyr when Mother and Father died."

A grayish tinge seeped beneath Jason's tan. "You want to run this place? You go ahead."

"Jason." Pearl clutched his arm.

He jerked his arm away. "Pearl and I and the kids will move into town. I've enough requests to bid on buildings now to give architecture a try. You go ahead and run this place by yourself. Run it into the ground for all I care."

"You'd like that, wouldn't you? It would prove you're the only Sterling son capable of running Dad's farm. Fine. If you want to leave, you go right ahead." Frank stormed to the door and grabbed his jacket from the wall pegs. Without waiting to put the jacket on, he left, slamming the door behind him so hard the house shook.

Except for the children's sobs, it was as though everyone had turned to stone. Frank's anger stunned Amy. She'd never seen his face twisted by fury before. *By pain.* The thought flashed through her mind. She knew instantly it was true—the anger was caused by incredible pain.

As Amy turned to hand Viola to Maggie, Pearl remonstrated with Jason, and Dan headed toward the door.

Amy touched Dan's sleeve. "I'll go." She reached for her coat and put it over her shoulders, not taking time to slip her arms into the sleeves.

Dan hesitated.

*He thinks I'm the last person Frank wants to see now,* she realized. "I won't stay if he chases me away."

"He's hurting."

His understanding of Frank and care for him warmed her heart. She was glad Frank had such a friend on the farm. "I know." She hurried out the door.

# eleven

Amy leaned against the wooden support and watched Frank currying a horse. Did the horse need it, she wondered, or did Frank simply need a way to release his angry energy without hurting himself and others?

She'd known he'd come to the animals he loved. She'd always appreciated the way he cared for animals. Their companionship comforted him, but today she wished he'd come to her for comfort instead.

"I thought I'd find you here," she said quietly.

Frank whirled. "What are you doing here?"

"Are you all right?" She crossed her arms over her chest, hugging herself beneath her jacket, wishing she could hug him instead.

"All right?" He made a sound that was half laugh and half sob. "Of course I'm all right. After all, the doctors said I was healed. They sent me home. I must be all right."

Shock stung her to silence. She struggled to keep her feelings from showing.

He raised his wounded arm. The sleeve hung flat and loose below the elbow. "Do you see a forearm and hand here? No? They're there in my dreams at night. They're there in my mind when I think about something I'm going to do. Know what's scariest? I feel them sometimes. Then I do things like I did today. I reach for something, and the truth throws itself in my face—and in everyone else's, too."

*That's what happened in the kitchen,* she realized. *Frank felt friendly and calm and ordinary. Then he reached for the glass, and the accident embarrassed him and reminded him of his wound, and the pain of it burst out in anger.*

Amy's throat ached with a sob that fought for release. *Don't let me cry, Lord. He needs me to be strong for him now.*

"Do you remember before the war, Amy, when I told you I had to fight? I still believe it's important to fight for other people's freedom. That's why I enlisted."

"I remember."

"That's not how I lost my arm, fighting for other people to be free."

"I don't understand."

"Did you read in the newspapers about the Filipino people? Like the Cubans, they fought the Spanish for their freedom."

She nodded. "The insurgents. They thought when we destroyed the Spanish fleet and forced Spain from the Philippines, they could reclaim control of their islands. Our government said no, that the Philippines are ours as the spoils of war."

"Right. So instead of fighting to free the Cubans, I fought to keep the Filipinos from gaining their freedom." The wild tone that had frightened Amy was gone.

She spoke cautiously. "Most Americans think the Philippine citizens did gain their freedom by becoming part of our free nation."

"During the Revolutionary War, the British felt the American colonists should be content to be part of Britain," Frank replied.

She couldn't argue with that.

"A lot of the men I fought beside hated the Filipinos. I don't think they hated them when we landed, but they grew to. They used nasty terms for them. They thought of the insurgents as lesser people, the way some white people still think of black people."

"How horrid."

"Yes, it is. At first I thought the men who felt that way were horrid, too. Then I realized many of them were only protecting themselves. Fighting the Filipinos went against everything they'd been raised to believe. The only way they could justify it was to find a way in their own minds to make the Filipinos wrong."

His understanding of his fellow soldiers amazed her and reminded her of all the reasons she loved him. She wished she dared tell him so.

He brushed his hand over his hair. "I can't even be angry at the Filipino responsible for my arm. He fought for his freedom. I was the one in the wrong, trying to keep that from him."

"Do you think God allowed you to lose your arm to punish you?"

"No. I don't know why God allowed it, but I don't think He was punishing me." Weariness weighted his words.

"God knows your heart, Frank." She walked slowly toward him. "He knows you joined the service to help people, not to take their freedom away. It's your heart God looks at."

A little of the strain in his face eased. "Thanks for reminding me."

Everything within her yearned to comfort him and help him heal. She rested her palm on his arm.

He jerked back. "Don't."

"I'm sorry." Rejection seared through her like a physical pain. "I only wanted. . .I hate to see you hurting like this."

He stepped away from her. His eyes looked emotionless. "I shouldn't have told you all that."

"Why not?"

"I didn't mean it as. . .as an invitation to renew our. . ."

"Our engagement?"

He nodded. "Go home, Amy."

"But—"

He raised his arm and let it drop against his side. "I don't know how to be only friends with you, and there's nowhere else for us to go anymore."

"There could be, if you weren't so stubborn. Life is never perfect for anyone, Frank. Can't you see that only makes it more important not to waste the gifts God gives us—those gifts that make the hard places easier and entire days bright and beautiful? Surely God wouldn't want us to waste our love for each other."

"I don't want to marry you."

Amy caught her breath. The words, so stark and cold, hit her like arrows. "I don't believe you." She blinked back sudden tears.

The muscles in his face tightened, but he said nothing.

"You think you aren't whole because you have only one arm. Don't you know neither of us will ever be whole until we're together, living as one as God intended?"

She spun about, not waiting for him to answer. Straw crunched beneath her shoes as she rushed through the barn and out into the bright, chill daylight. Tears tumbled after each other down her cheeks as she hurried to the farmhouse. In the kitchen, she grabbed her things, aware of the Sterlings watching her in stunned silence. She hurt too much to care what they must think.

On the way back to town, her mind replayed the conversation with Frank. Then she remembered another conversation with Frank when he had said, "I'm not the man I was before I went to war. The war changed me."

She'd told him it couldn't change him. But maybe it had. Today he'd revealed a tiny piece of what he experienced in the war. What he chose to not reveal must be horrendous. How did a man live with the memories of war?

"Please, Lord, heal his heart and bring him peace."

It was her constant prayer. How could he possibly return to her if he didn't heal?

*What if God heals him, but Frank doesn't return to me?*

Amy caught her breath at the thought. It didn't seem possible Frank wouldn't want to spend his life with her if his heart healed. They'd loved each other for so many years. Surely he couldn't ever love another woman.

What if he could? She forced herself to face the possibility. Would she want his heart healed if it meant he spent his life with someone else? "Yes, Lord," she whispered. "Please heal him, even if You use the love of another woman to do so."

"But. . .what about love hoping all things, Lord?" Her question brought a rueful smile. Already she was trying to convince God to only heal Frank in a way that brought him back to a life with her.

God didn't force people into His will. He didn't force them to love Him. She couldn't expect God to force Frank to come back to her, either. Part of loving someone was allowing them to make their own choices.

"If he doesn't come back, what will I do?" For a moment, all she could picture was an empty future. She took a deep breath and brushed at a stray tear. A lot of women lived without the men they loved. There were a number of widows in Chippewa City. Some retreated into lives made up of nothing but self-pity. Most built useful lives. They gave their love to their family and neighbors. They might miss the one they loved, but they found life still had beautiful and bountiful places.

*I can do that, too. I have more than most women. I've my painting and teaching, in addition to Father and my friends.* Gratitude eased the constriction in her chest from the separation from Frank. Amy lifted her chin and threw a promise out on the breeze. "I'm not going to waste this life, God. I'm not going to let my heart shrivel up because Frank won't marry me. I'm going to make a fine life with the gifts You've given me."

Maybe Frank would never return to her, but God wouldn't leave.

*At least Frank is alive,* she thought. She tugged on the

reins, and the horse stopped. She removed her left glove and watched sunlight play over the ruby heart in her ring. Slowly she pulled the ring from her finger. "I love you, Frank. I'll always love you. If you can't heal with me in your life, I'll accept that. But please let the Lord help you heal, whatever it takes." Amy opened her reticule and dropped the ring inside.

❧

Frank set the kerosene lamp he'd carried down from his bedroom on the kitchen table, then walked over to the window. Staring out at the mist-shrouded moon, he sighed and leaned his forehead against the cold glass. He felt weary to his bones.

His mind drifted back to Amy and their conversation in the barn. His heart savored the love she'd showed him. What kept her loving him? He'd been cold toward her for months, and she never retaliated in kind. She only kept loving him.

It frightened him the way his anger had exploded today. He could still see his family's shocked faces and hear the children crying. He loved those children. More than anyone else, they'd accepted him as whole when he returned with his wounded arm. Chalmers had been open in his curiosity and questions about the arm, but he never acted like the injury made Frank a freak. He hated that he'd frightened the children.

"Forgive me, Lord. Help me never to let my anger get out of control like that again."

Years ago when he drank heavily, before he decided to live as he believed Christ would want, he'd fought with Jason. It seemed he'd been angry all the time back then. His anger today reminded him of those times. That he hadn't physically harmed anyone was only slight consolation.

The explosion reinforced his conviction that Amy was better off without him.

At a sound behind him, he turned. It was Dan. "You couldn't sleep, either?"

Dan stretched his arms over his head. "No."

"The nightmares again?"

"Yep. You, too?"

"No. Not tonight."

Nightmares from the war disturbed their sleep more nights than either liked to admit. They'd wondered aloud to each other whether the dark dreams would ever leave them for good. It seemed a man should at least have sleep to escape life's horrors. Neither of the men told the others in the house about the dreams. They didn't speak of the war much to others at all—not the true war. They shared funny or interesting sidelights. The things of nightmares remained only between them.

Dan leaned against the wall next to the window and crossed his arms over his chest. "You had an interesting day."

Frank shrugged.

"Wasn't like you to argue so fiercely with your brother. I'd have thought you'd seen enough fighting in the Philippines to last you a lifetime. Guess I was wrong. You came back home to fight with your family and the girl you love."

"I thought you'd understand." Frank didn't look at his friend. "Their lives are so different from ours." He pointed to his temple. "In here."

"So you push your family out of your life. Are you trying to prove you don't need them?"

"I'm not trying to prove anything."

"Is it such an awful thing to need people? Everyone needs others, even people with both arms."

"I didn't say— "

"God put us in a world filled with people. Do you think He did that so we'd be alone? I think He did it because He means for us to lean on each other and work together. You and your brothers are running a farm here, raising crops to feed people. That's a noble calling. Isn't it worth working together?"

"I don't have any choice but to lean on others, thanks to this arm."

"What about Amy?"

Frank swung around and settled his hand on his hip. "You're sticking your nose way too far into my business."

"You and I have been through more together than most people. We've always spoken the truth to each other. I'm not planning to stop now. If you don't like it, you can send me packing along with everyone else in your life."

Frank sighed and wiped his hand over his face. "No."

"So, what about Amy?"

"What about her?"

"You've admitted to me you still love her. I know you think you're doing her a favor stepping out of her life, but she obviously doesn't see it that way."

"She's better off without me."

Dan shook his head. "Amy isn't the kind of woman to quit loving you because you lost part of your arm. You do her a disservice if you think she is." He pushed himself away from the wall. "I'd give anything in my power to have my wife back for just one day or even five minutes. I wouldn't love her one iota less if she came back missing an arm." He started toward the stairway door. "Good night."

"It's not the arm."

Dan turned around. "What?"

Frank took a deep breath. "I said, it's not the arm. I didn't know that until tonight. All this time, I thought it was the arm. I thought I was doing the honorable thing, not burdening Amy with a crippled husband." He told Dan what he'd shared with Amy in the barn. "Tonight I started thinking about the nightmares and all the other things you and I don't talk about. That's when I realized my arm is like. . .like a symbol, always reminding me of how much I've changed inside. I'm not the same person I was when I left for the war."

"None of us are."

"Do you think it's fair to Amy to marry her like this, while I have nightmares when I'm asleep and nightmares when I'm awake?"

"She loves you. She'd be good for you."

"I wouldn't be good for her. I appreciate your advice on most things, but Amy is off-limits from now on."

They stared at each other. Finally Dan spoke. "All right."

Frank breathed deeply in relief. He didn't want to argue with his friend. "Did I ever tell you about the dream I had in the hospital?"

"The nightmares?"

"No, just the opposite. In this dream you and I were walking down a path together. Christ walked with us, larger than life, His arms spread out as though to guard and bless us. We were surrounded by the most intense sense of peace."

Dan was smiling by the time Frank finished describing the dream. "I'll take that dream over a nightmare any time."

"I didn't know what to make of the dream at first, the part about you and me together. You were still in the Philippines. I was in a hospital in the States. Didn't know if we'd ever see each other again. Now here you are, standing by me closer than any of my old friends. Maybe that's what Christ meant to show me, that both of you would. . .you know. Sometimes I think you're the only one who understands what I've been through."

"That goes both ways. Besides, with Christ walking alongside, a man can handle a heap of hard places."

"You've said something there." Frank straightened. "Guess I've put myself in a harder place than necessary, all but kicking my brother off the farm."

Dan grinned. "You might say."

"I've been home three months. I think it's time I stop wallowing around in self-pity. Are you planning to stick it out with me here on the farm?"

"Just try to get rid of me."

"Then let's start rebuilding our lives. From this point on, when one of us starts slipping into discouragement, the other shores him up."

"Sounds good to me."

"You may do more than your share of shoring up."

Dan shrugged. "I doubt it. Life has a way of evening things like that out. For now, I suggest we try to get some sleep. Dawn won't wait on us."

As they climbed the stairs together, Frank reflected on the part of the dream he hadn't shared with Dan. Frank had been walking between Dan and Amy. Christ's arms had encompassed them all.

*Am I walking away from a blessing God intends for me by walking away from Amy,* Frank wondered, *just like she accused me of doing today?*

# twelve

Amy turned from the pharmacy counter with a packet of headache powders for her father in her hand. A familiar image stood silhouetted against the sunlit window at the front of the store. She hurried toward him. "Hello, Jason."

"Hello, Amy." He smiled and pushed back his broad-brimmed gray felt hat. "What are you doing out in this weather with nothing but that shawl for protection? Don't you know it's winter?"

"I only ran down for some headache powders."

"I forgot you live upstairs."

"Pearl told me you and the family are moving into town this week."

He nodded. "Yes. We moved in yesterday. Renting a house at the top of the hill. It's a bit small for all of us, but we can make do for awhile."

She struggled to maintain composure. "I know Frank's accusations angered you, but I didn't think you meant it when you said you'd leave the farm. Jason, how could you leave him alone out there?"

"He's not alone. Dan Terrell is staying with him."

"Only two men for the entire farm. You know it's too much for Frank."

The smile with which he'd greeted her was gone. "Frank and Dan will get along fine. Frank and I apologized to each other the day after our argument. When I threw out the idea of moving to town, it was just anger talking. But the more I thought about it, the more I thought it was a good idea."

"But—"

He lifted a hand to silence her. "The only way Frank is going to learn to rely on himself is if he's forced into it. Without all of us around, he won't be embarrassed when he can't handle something the first time. Since it's winter, he can take most things at his own pace."

"You honestly believe he can do it, that he can be a farmer on his own?"

"With some hired help, I think he has a good chance. He's a natural-born farmer, Amy. He knows when it's time to plant just by the feel and smell of the soil. Sometimes I think he knows what the animals are thinking. If he doesn't have me and Andy to lean on, he'll see for himself that he can handle it. You'll see."

She hoped he was right. Frustration made her feel restless. Frank seemed bent on making life more difficult than necessary, pushing away everyone who loved him.

"You're the only one left who can help him, God," she whispered, climbing the steps to the apartment.

❧

Amy stood before an easel in the academy studio where she taught, admiring the painting of a student from her last class. The young man had caught the elusive quality of shadow moving across a field of grain. Only another painter would know the difficulty in capturing that.

The student was easily the most talented she'd worked with. He'd never worked with oils before her class. It thrilled her to know she'd helped bring out his God-given talent.

"Miss Henderson?"

"Yes?" Amy turned toward the door, expecting a male student behind the respectful inquiry. Instead Dan Terrell stood in the doorway, broad-brimmed felt hat in hand. "Mr. Terrell, this is a surprise. Do come in." She darted a glance about at the room and laughed. "There's nowhere clean to offer you to sit down, I'm afraid."

"I've never been in a place where people paint pictures before." His gaze moved about the room slowly. "It's fascinating. Must be nice to work in a room with huge windows like this. Is the smell of paint always this strong?"

"No. We're working with oil paints right now. Sometimes we work with watercolors or just sketching. Does the smell bother you? It does some people. I can open a window if you'd like, or we can go out in the hall to talk."

"No, it doesn't bother me." He grinned. "As to opening a window, I had enough fresh Minnesota December air riding into town."

She returned his grin. "And what brought you here, Mr. Terrell?"

"I came to pay you for the painting. Meant to pay you when you brought it out to the farm, but. . ." He hesitated, worrying the brim of his hat.

Embarrassment tightened Amy's chest at the remembrance of that afternoon. She forced herself to meet his gaze. "But I rushed off."

"Yes. Anyway, here's the money." He dug it out of his pocket and handed it to her. "Doesn't seem nearly enough for what that painting means to me."

"I'm glad you like it, Mr. Terrell." Without counting it, she dropped the money into a pocket on the front of the white painting smock she wore to protect her shirtwaist and navy blue skirt. "I'm sorry about your wife. How long ago. . .when did the accident happen?"

"Two years ago. Still have a hard time believing it."

"I understand that."

His gaze searched hers. "I think you do." He took a deep breath and began worrying his hat brim again. "About that afternoon at the farm. . .I know it's none of my business, but there's something I'd like to say."

Trepidation sent a warning along her nerves. "I'm not sure—"

"Please, Miss. Let me start. Then if you don't want to hear what I'm saying, ask me to stop and I will."

"All right." She slid her hands into the pockets of her smock.

"Frank's a good man, Miss Henderson."

Amy smiled. "We agree on that."

"What I mean to say is, it's not like him to get so riled as he did with Jason. Sometimes he just doesn't know what to do with all the pain that's built up inside him."

She nodded. "I know. I haven't always understood that. I think Frank learned a long time ago, when he stopped drinking, that pain makes people do things that seem unkind or unwise. He told me that years ago. I tried to understand it then, but I don't think I did completely until he came back from the war."

Dan's shoulders lowered a bit at her response, as though some tension went out of them. "He's got a whale of a lot of healing to do, Miss, and I don't just mean his arm. War leaves a lot of nasty pictures in a man's mind and a lot of questions." He heaved a sigh. "War throws strange bedfellows together. Frank and I fought alongside rich men, poor men, fine men, and not so fine men. One of the men in our regiment belongs to one of the richest families in St. Paul. Bryant's his name. Couldn't find a better fellow if you searched the entire earth. Did Frank tell you how he lost his arm?"

Amy frowned, trying to follow his quick change of subjects. "No. He never offered to, and I never had the courage to ask him to relive the experience."

"There was a soldier in the Thirteenth who didn't like Frank. Didn't like me much, either, but he especially didn't like Frank. Name was Elias Goodworth." Dan shook his head. "Misnomer if I ever heard one."

"Why didn't he like Frank?"

Dan shrugged. "Not sure exactly. It started when he

discovered Frank and I don't drink. He'd make comments about how if we couldn't handle a stiff drink we weren't manly enough to be decent soldiers. We never bothered retaliating. At first some of the other men snickered at Goodworth's comments. Eventually, most of the men learned that Frank and I weren't shirkers when it came to fighting, and they quit joining in Goodworth's sarcasm."

"I should think so."

"During one battle, Goodworth was close to Frank and me. Frank was only a yard or so away from him. An insurgent—that's one of the Filipinos we were fighting—seemed to come out of nowhere. He lunged toward Goodworth, his sword drawn. Goodworth didn't even see him. Frank dove for Goodworth. Shoved him out of the way. The Filipino's sword came down full force on Frank's arm."

Amy gasped. She crossed her arms over her chest in a sudden movement, as if to protect herself from the pain that lashed her.

"Far as I know, Goodworth's never even thanked Frank. But Frank's never once spoken ill of Goodworth."

"Frank told me he couldn't be angry with the Filipino, that the man was only fighting for his freedom. Frank never mentioned Mr. Goodworth."

"I expect there's a lot he hasn't mentioned to you. I know he loves you. He's afraid if he marries you, he'll bring all the pain he's dealing with right into the marriage with him. He doesn't think that's fair to you." Dan's smile was reflected in his eyes. "I think you're a strong enough lady to handle that. I expect he thinks so, too, but he loves you too much to want you to have to face his problems."

"Isn't that what love is for?"

Dan stared at the floor. "That's exactly what Belinda would have said." His voice was soft. He swallowed hard before continuing. "I'm afraid Frank has a long way to go before he will let himself admit how much he loves and needs you. I'm not sure he ever will."

She nodded slowly. Pain filled her chest until it felt her rib cage must burst from it. "Thank you for telling me about. . . about how Frank. . ."

"Sure. Frank might not appreciate the way I'm sticking my nose in here, but I thought you had a right to know."

"I'm glad you're his friend. He needs someone now, and he won't let me or his family close."

"He trusts me because I was there. I saw what he saw. I have the same memories. I came back with both arms intact, but a lot of things I still need to figure out, just like Frank." He told her briefly about the nightmares.

Footsteps and cheerful voices in the hall caught Amy's attention. "I'm afraid my next class starts in a few minutes."

Dan straightened his shoulders. "I'll be going then."

"Thank you for coming. It means a great deal to me to know these things about Frank. I'll know better how to pray for him now."

Dan lowered his voice as students began entering the room. "I'm not sure he will let himself come back to you."

Amy heard the regret in his voice. It echoed in her heart. "I know, but at least I understand him better."

She tucked the revelations away in her heart to reflect on later and turned to bring order to the class.

❧

Frank slung the T-stool into the straw, sat down on it, and began milking the brown-and-white cow. "Sorry the job goes so slow with only one hand, Sudsy."

"Me-eow."

Frank glanced over his shoulder but continued to milk. The one-eyed golden tabby cat balanced on top of the stall wall. "Careful, Gideon. You know you have a habit of forgetting you can't see on the side you're missing that eye. You've fallen off that wall more times than I've seen Christmas."

Frank turned his attention back to the cow, relaxing to the rhythmic hissing of the milk into the pail.

Gideon jumped down from the wall to Frank's shoulder.

Frank laughed. "I'm not going to squirt any milk your way while you're up there." He brushed his cheek against the cat's. "You haven't let living with one eye get you down, have you, Fella? You're the best mouser on the farm. Think I'll learn to handle living with one arm as well as you've learned to live with one eye? At least Dan's standing by me this winter."

Although he'd lived on a farm all his life, everything seemed new to Frank now. Chores he could practically do in his sleep before the war needed his full attention to perform with one hand. On some days, things as simple as tying a knot could make him so frustrated he wanted to give up farming for good.

Dan stood by him through all the struggles. "Nothing lost," he'd say when Frank couldn't get something right the first time. "Try again."

Dan pulled his own weight, but he never jumped in to do things for Frank without first giving Frank a chance to try them himself.

Initially, Frank had been terrified. For all he'd harangued Jason, accusing him of taking responsibility for the farm away from him, Frank discovered he was scared to death at trying to run it himself.

As the months passed, Frank grew more competent at performing the chores. And as his abilities grew, his frustration at the world dissipated. Work didn't knock the stuffing out of him the way it had when he'd just gotten out of the hospital. Instead it was building back the muscles he'd lost.

The first time he lifted a sack of feed that would have taken him two hands to lift before the war, the realization sent a jolt of elation through him. He laughed out loud and looked in wonder at the sleeve stretched tight over his bulging muscles. *I can't wait to show Amy,* he thought. Instead he kept the news to himself and was rewarded by Dan's comment two weeks later on his growing strength.

It helped that Frank had only the relatively easy chores of winter to do as he began rebuilding his strength. Caring for the livestock, cleaning the barn and stables, repairing and cleaning tools and equipment, and going through seed catalogs with Dan filled most of his waking hours. Learning to ride a horse and handle a team while driving a wagon was a challenge that at first frightened, then excited him as he became more accomplished.

Often as Frank worked, Dan's words about the importance of farming came back to him. Frank found it healing to his soul to think of his work as something that blessed others.

The frequency of those times when nightmares woke him with racing pulse, drenched in sweat, decreased. As he began to trust in his physical abilities and began to see beauty in the world again, he discovered himself clinging to new hope: the hope that Amy was right about him, the hope that beneath all the things he'd seen and experienced in the war was a man who at the center was kind and good and strong in Christ.

But as far as Frank could tell, his heart hadn't healed at all. Amy was still the first person he thought of when he awakened and the last thought on his mind at night.

He and Dan celebrated Christmas in town at the house Jason and Pearl were renting. Seeing Amy at the Christmas Eve service was especially painful. Later that night he shared with Dan the story of a Christmas Eve years earlier.

"When I first asked Amy to court me, I'd just decided to live for Christ. I'd been drinking and gambling pretty heavy for awhile before that. I was making a new start. Amy's father didn't trust my change of heart. He said Amy couldn't see me until I proved I was a changed man by not drinking or gambling for a year. I was crushed. Then Amy said she believed in me, and we'd celebrate my success by attending the Christmas Eve service together when the year was over."

"And did you?"

"Yes." Images of that night drifted through his mind. The pleasure of her faith in him and of that evening together filled him with the joy of the love they'd shared, and he smiled. "Her faith in me helped me through a lot of tempting times that year. I used to compare that year to Jacob's years of work to earn the right to marry Rachel. Remember that Old Testament story?"

"I do. Sounds like you and Amy have been through a lot together."

"Yes."

"Maybe too much to throw it all away?"

Frank grinned. "Maybe I talk too much. Did you hear Professor Headley tonight?"

"That's a pretty abrupt change of subject."

Frank ignored the jibe. "The professor asked if I'd give some classes on agriculture and livestock. He said there are so many young men in the area going into farming—men who can't afford to learn the latest methods at the university like I did—that this might be a good way to share my knowledge."

"I think that's a great idea."

"So do I. At least until spring, when there's so much to do around the farm."

It would also give him a reason to be near Amy. Frank wasn't ready to change his mind about their future, but it would be nice to see her more often. Just to be around her would be a blessing.

Even in his daily Scripture readings he was reminded of her. Sometimes it seemed he couldn't open the Bible without his gaze lighting on a reference to married love. He hadn't realized before that there were so many such verses.

He became aware of them first when he opened to Proverbs 31 and read how blessed a man is who has a virtuous wife, "for her price is far above rubies." The comparison to rubies, the stone in the ring he'd given Amy, only made the words cut quicker to his heart.

Seeing two cows huddled together against the chill winter winds one afternoon reminded him of the verses in the fourth chapter of Ecclesiastes he'd read the night before: "Two are better than one; because they have a good reward for their labour. For if they fall, the one will lift up his fellow: but woe to him that is alone when he falleth; for he hath not another to help him up. Again, if two lie together, then they have heat: but how can one be warm alone? And if one prevail against him, two shall withstand him; and a threefold cord is not quickly broken."

It brought back the memory of Amy's theory that their love for each other was a gift from God to make the hard places in their lives easier.

Were the Bible verses he kept coming across a coincidence? Was God trying to push him back to Amy?

The verse that struck him most forcefully was Proverbs 18:22: "Whoso findeth a wife findeth a good thing, and obtaineth favour of the Lord." Frank's immediate thought was that finding Amy had indeed been a very good thing. His second was that obtaining favor of the Lord sounded like a good thing, too.

His third was that he didn't believe that finding him had necessarily been a good thing for Amy. Marrying might be good for him, but it would definitely not be good for her.

❧

Frank hummed a popular tune as he hurried through Windom Academy in early March, headed for the hall where Amy's picture of the returning soldier hung. Ever since he started teaching at the academy, he'd avoided the painting, though his heart had longed to see it again. It was a tangible reminder of the love Amy had once held for him. His mind warned him that seeing it would only open him to more pain.

His heart won out.

He stepped into the large hall and stopped short. His heart slammed against his rib cage. Amy stood before the picture. While he watched, she reached up and removed it from the wall.

Running into her hadn't been part of his plan. They saw each other often at the academy. That was inevitable. But usually there were students or other faculty members around. It was nice being near her, seeing her laugh or her eyes warm in sympathy with another or sparkle in excitement with a shared idea. Still, he never sought her out alone.

Now he took a step back, hoping to slip away undetected. Instead he bumped into the door.

Amy looked over her shoulder. "Hello, Frank."

He gave up the retreat and walked toward her. The sadness in her eyes grabbed at his heart. Did she see the same thing in his eyes, the regret that they weren't together? He pulled his gaze away and indicated the picture she was holding with a nod of his head. "Taking it down?"

"I'm taking it home." She laid it face down on two pieces of cotton-wrapped wood. "The war is over."

"Yes." He supposed for most people it was over. He wondered if it would ever be entirely over for him. "People are ready to move on." Like he and Dan were trying to do.

"Some people, anyway." Amy pulled the cotton ties from the wood protectors behind the back of the picture and secured them.

Was she indicating that she wasn't ready to move on? More likely she thought he was not moving on.

He watched while she wrapped a large piece of white cotton around the painting and tied it in place with twine. Pain sliced through him when he saw she no longer wore the ruby-heart ring he'd given her before leaving for war. Immediately he reprimanded himself. What kind of fool was he to think she'd wear the symbol of his love for her the rest of her life? Isn't this what he wanted, for her to leave them behind the way the war must be left behind?

"I hope you're enjoying teaching," Amy said. "The students are enthusiastic about your classes."

The knowledge sent a thrill through him. "Glad to hear it. I hoped they'd find the classes useful, but you never know."

The smile he knew so well lit her face. "Yes. It's like that for all of us."

It was nice, knowing they shared this experience. "The students speak highly of your classes, too. And of you."

"Thank you for telling me. Teaching is a great blessing to me." Amy picked up her gray, thigh-length wool coat with maroon trim from a nearby table and started to put it on.

"Let me help you with that." Frank grabbed one shoulder of the coat. Surprise jolted through him. He'd forgotten for a moment he had only one hand. He couldn't hold the coat properly. For all his improvement in handling farm chores and animals, helping a woman into a coat made him feel awkward and inadequate.

Amy didn't appear to notice. She managed to slip her arms inside the sleeves with grace.

The light floral fragrance she wore wafted to him. He'd forgotten that such close proximity held that pleasure.

She turned around. "Do you mind if we talk for a minute?"

"I thought that's what we were doing."

"I mean about us."

"Amy—"

"I won't beg you to come back to us, I promise."

Is that how she thought of them, not as two separate people in love with each other but as one unit called *us?* Funny how right that felt to him, even though he'd torn that unit apart. "All right. What did you want to say?"

She took a deep, shaky breath. "I want to thank you for all the beautiful things you brought into my life. You taught me so much about love—not only love between a man and a woman but love for others."

"I taught you?" He smiled. "You are the most loving, gentle, strong woman I know. I'm sure you taught me more than I taught you."

"No. Years ago, after you'd given up drinking, you told me that men who drank heavily weren't evil; they were only trying to heal some deep pain in their lives. I tried to understand, truly I did. A few months ago you told me a little bit of what you face because of the war, and I began to understand more about the wounded places inside people."

"I don't want—"

Amy touched the palm of her hand to the front of his jacket. "I know you don't want to talk about those wounds. I'm not asking you to. I'm only trying to say that because of you, I think I understand God's love better. I think I'm a more loving person. I want you to know that I treasure that gift from you."

Her revelation overwhelmed him. "I don't know what to say."

"You needn't say anything."

He watched in silence while she pulled on her gloves, pinned on a small maroon hat, and wrapped a plush maroon muffler around her neck.

She picked up the picture.

He reached for it. "I'll carry it for you."

She hesitated.

Anger flashed through him. Resignation followed. He'd told Dan once that the missing arm was only a symbol of the changes inside him. It was a symbol, but not *only* a symbol. He chose not to act from his anger. He purposefully softened his voice. "It's all right, Amy. I won't drop your painting. My arm is a lot stronger now."

She allowed him to take it. "Thank you. I didn't think you'd harm it."

He mentally kicked himself. He should have known her concern wasn't for the painting.

They walked together in silence through the building to the front door. Outside, a horse and buggy were tied at a hitching post near the bottom of the stone steps. "Professor Headley is letting me borrow his horse and buggy to take the painting home," Amy explained. "I hitched up the horse before going to get the painting. I'm becoming quite accomplished at hitching and unhitching. I'm quite proud of myself." She beamed.

"You should be." He beamed back at her, finding pleasure in her excitement at mastering the task he'd learned to perform almost before he could remember.

Wind swept across the snow-covered prairie and pulled Amy's maroon plush muffler into a banner. It yanked Frank's hat from his head. It danced and rolled along the ground. "Hey!" Carrying the painting, he couldn't retrieve the hat.

Amy ran after it, making three futile grabs before capturing it. They laughed together as she placed it back on his head and tightened the cord, which he seldom used, beneath his chin.

The closeness of her laughing eyes and the lips that had shared kisses with him so many times was painfully sweet. He wanted to pull her close and hold her forever. If his hand wasn't clutching the picture between them, he might give in to the temptation to do just that, he realized.

Amy's laughter died. Her hands rested on his shoulders. "Why do you think. . ."

"Why do I think what?"

"Why do you think our love was put through so many tests? We went through so much and waited such a long time to be together. Then the war came and destroyed everything."

"I don't know, Amy." He wished he could make the sadness in her eyes go away. He didn't know how to do that without asking her to marry him again, and he was certain that wasn't the right thing to do. He didn't even have two arms to hold her anymore.

He broke the invisible cords binding them together and put the picture in the buggy. He steadied her as she climbed up into the buggy. "Be careful, Amy. The roads are still pretty rough with ice and snow."

"I'll be careful."

He watched the buggy start down the road across the plateau toward town, the wind whipping the horse's mane in a picturesque dance. "Take care of her, Lord. Make her happy."

His fanciful thoughts wondered whether the wind carried his prayer heavenward.

❧

Amy forced herself to keep her attention on the road, though everything within her urged her to look back at Frank. Was he watching her drive away? When they were courting, he always watched until she was out of sight. She'd done the same when he'd left her.

She both loved and hated that Frank worked at the academy. He only taught two courses, and his classes didn't meet every day, so at least he wasn't around constantly. It was painful seeing him so often when he chose for them not to be together. It was nice to look across the tables at lunch and see his eyes light up while he talked with faculty or students. Was it her imagination, or was he truly growing in confidence, learning he wasn't only his body, that he had so much to offer others?

Whenever she found herself begging God to bring Frank back to her, she made herself stop. "God has a plan for my life, with or without Frank," she'd told Pearl. "It's still hard to believe we'll never be together again, but sometime I'll get used to it."

"Have you seen anyone else?" Pearl had asked.

"No."

"I can't believe none of Chippewa City's young men have come around."

"A few have asked to escort me on occasion," Amy admitted. "I'm not ready to replace Frank yet. My heart still feels bruised. For now I'm spending my time with Father or my work and once in awhile helping out your father."

Dr. Matt had asked her to do simple nursing for patients on occasion since her experience at Camp Ramsey and Fort Snelling. At first she'd felt her training wasn't adequate, but he assured her he would not ask anything of her that was beyond her ability. Mostly she helped care for older patients, allowing their families some time to rest. It was rewarding work. And it helped fill her time and keep her from feeling sorry for herself.

"Maybe getting to know some other men would be a good idea," Pearl suggested in a gentle manner. "You wouldn't need to fall in love with someone else right away."

Amy laughed. "As though one plans such a thing." Her smile died. "I think I need to heal from Frank's leaving a bit more first."

Maybe Pearl was right, Amy reflected as she pulled the horse to a stop in front of the pharmacy and her home. Maybe the only way she would ever rout Frank from her heart was by making the commitment to allow another man to fill his place. But she wasn't ready for that yet. She expected it would be a long time before she was ready for another love.

# thirteen

Frank opened the top drawer of the mahogany desk in the parlor and looked down at the yellowing newspaper pages. Pearl had tried to get him to look at them before she and Jason left the farm, but Frank had refused. The pages contained articles about Camp Ramsey and Fort Snelling during the time Amy spent there. Pictures Amy had sketched of life in the camps and hospitals were included in some of the articles.

He hadn't dared open his heart to the pain of looking at the clippings before today. The short time he'd spent with Amy in the snow in front of Windom Academy had renewed his longing to know more about what she'd experienced. Maybe the fact that her painting of the returning soldier was no longer available for him to see whenever he chose had sparked the interest.

He lit the hanging lamp with its globe of painted roses and sat in the plush green chair beneath it, clippings in hand. He read every word, examined every sketch of army life and patient life in the camps, imagined Amy in the midst of it all with the sick and dying soldiers. And let the tears fall.

❧

By the end of March, spring began to show its face on the Minnesota prairie. Snow showers spattered occasionally across the land, but for the most part they were short-lived and often mixed with rain. Prairie roosters boomed announcements of spring's promise from ridges at sunrise and sunset, and prairie hens responded with excited squawks.

As much as Frank enjoyed teaching at the academy, he was glad to return to the fields. Walking behind the team working the harrow tested his mettle. There were no handles to grasp, only the reins. He and Dan had worked hard with the horses during the winter months, teaching them to respond to verbal commands in addition to the urging of reins. It paid off now in spades. Frank's heels dug into the soft, turned soil as he trudged back and forth across the fields. The work left his arm and calves stiff, but his spirit soared. Wonderful, to face a challenge like this and conquer it.

More than once he fell in the conquering. While walking behind the drag, his heels would slip in the moist earth or the horses would jerk him off balance, and he'd land on the ground. At first the falls frustrated him. Then he remembered that he'd had many similar falls in the fields before the war. Everything couldn't be blamed on his arm.

On beautiful spring days, he felt sorry for the people working in cities. He loved watching spring unfold into summer. The prairie sky, which so many thought of as empty, was filled with ducks and geese making their way north, followed by the crane. The birds' cries added to the joy of the day.

Frank swallowed his pride and asked Andy to help on the farm. He was pleased that Andy quickly agreed. When Jason offered to help out, too, Frank could have leaped with joy. Instead he merely nodded and said, "I'd appreciate that."

"I can't work every day," Jason qualified. "I've my other work to do, but it doesn't take up all my time yet."

"Farm still belongs to all of us," Frank reminded him. "Up to you whether you choose to work it or not, though I'd be glad for your help."

"I hope one day to be able to support my family working as an architect. Maybe when that day comes, you'll want to buy my part of the farm."

"We'll talk about it when and if the time comes."

It felt strange at first to have his brothers turn to him as the leader at the farm. They knew what needed to be done, but

Frank was the one who determined who did what and when on a daily basis.

Wheat was sown first, early, when the chill was barely out of the ground. Corn was sown next. The earth changed daily, the fields and meadows growing greener and more lush until in June the land pulsated with life everywhere: crops, prairie grass, fragrant wild flowers, birds, grasshoppers, chirping crickets, flies, mosquitoes, and prairie dogs.

As Frank worked, verses from Ecclesiastes repeated in his mind day after day. "To every thing there is a season, and a time to every purpose under heaven: a time to be born, and a time to die; a time to plant, and a time to pluck up that which is planted."

One evening, over biscuits and salt pork, Frank told Dan, "I feel like one of those hard kernels of seed corn. They look as dead as I felt when I returned from the war. Now they're green plants growing taller every day, filled with life, able to bend before the wind. I'm beginning to feel alive again, too."

All his life, working the land, he'd watched spring and summer follow fall and winter. He knew from the watching that God always brought a form of life out of every kind of death. Frank began to feel the stirrings of excitement within his chest. What would his new life look like?

Some things would never change. Some wounds would take years to heal, and their scars would always remain. Challenges would continually need to be faced. But there was beauty in the world, and strength was returning to his body and soul.

"For awhile I thought life would never be good again," he admitted to Dan. "Now I know it will be."

*Even without Amy,* he admitted to himself.

Frank was delighted one day by the sight of a red fox racing out of the cornfield and across the road, its tail flying straight out behind it. The beauty of the creature delighted him.

He remembered his father telling him as a boy that an injured fox hid away by itself until it healed.

*That's what I've been doing,* he realized with sudden clarity. He'd withdrawn from the world as much as possible to heal the wounds left from the war. A hope he hadn't allowed himself before stirred within him. Maybe one day he'd be healed enough to allow Amy back into his life. If she still wanted him by then.

❧

Amy awoke smiling. Morning sunshine softly reached through lace curtains to brighten her bedchamber. Mourning doves cooed from the ledge outside her window. She stretched luxuriously, still wrapped in the sense of peace and joy she'd felt in her dream.

Closing her eyes, she recaptured the images from her sleep world. She and Frank walked along a path. Between them walked Christ, holding their hands. Everything was bright.

Did the dream mean Christ was bringing her and Frank together again? That was the hope her heart leaped to first.

Maybe the dream meant that although they weren't together—for Christ was between them—Christ walked with them both. Surely that was true regardless of whether she and Frank spent the rest of their lives together. This morning, feeling the peace and joy in Christ's presence in the dream, Amy knew it was enough that He walked with each of them, wherever life led.

❧

One day in mid-June, Frank was surprised to receive a letter from a man he'd fought beside. "It's from Timothy Bryant," he told Dan, tearing open the envelope.

He scanned the letter quickly. A thrill darted through him. "He's coming out this way. Plans to be here for the Fourth of July."

"What's a city man like him want out here on the prairie?"

"Says he's planning to run for a congressional seat this year. Wants to get in some stomping this summer. Wants to start here with the Fourth celebration. Then take in the fairs in late summer."

"Not a bit surprised he's interested in politics."

"Wants to stay with us when he comes out. It will be good to see him again."

Timothy Bryant arrived the Saturday before the Fourth. The three former soldiers sat up late into the night reminiscing. It surprised Frank to realize all the memories weren't filled with horror. There had been times of camaraderie and humor, too.

And the war had brought good friends into his life. Bryant, born to an affluent Minneapolis family, wouldn't be in Frank's home, acting as comfortable as one of his farmer neighbors, if it weren't for the war.

Dan showed Timothy the picture Amy had painted.

"This is very well done," Timothy praised. "Who is the artist?"

"Amy Henderson. You remember the girl Frank was always talking about, don't you?" Dan asked, grinning at Frank.

Frank frowned at him.

Timothy turned to Frank. "I'm surprised to find such talent out here on the prairie. Where did she study?"

"She took some classes at the University of Minnesota in St. Paul."

Timothy studied the picture closer. "I know a thing or two about painting. My parents have quite a collection of work by the finer artists. I'd like to see more of your Amy's work."

"She isn't my Amy." Frank darted a look of disgust at Dan. "But I think she'll agree to let you see more of her paintings. I'll ask her tomorrow."

The 1900 Fourth of July celebration planned by the county was the most elaborate Frank could remember. The county fathers were bent on celebrating the United States' expansion of its manifest destiny with the addition of Hawaii and the Philippines. Frank wasn't so sure that expansion was the country's destiny. He was surprised when Reverend Conrad asked him to speak at church the Sunday before the Fourth. He tried to decline.

"I've nothing worth saying. I know some of the townspeople consider me a war hero, but I'm not."

"Speak to them about what you told me, about the healing. It's not only wounded soldiers who need to heal from the war, you know. The whole country needs to heal, whether we admit it or not."

That's how Frank found himself preaching one-half of the sermon on Sunday morning. Reverend Conrad had been part of Chippewa City since the town began. Frank felt Reverend Conrad's introduction was a sermon in itself.

"Chippewa City is a babe as towns go. It's only thirty-odd years old. It grew from scratch here on the prairie at the meeting of the Minnesota and Chippewa Rivers after the Sioux were forced to leave this land. We struggled with growing pains, the same as our nation has struggled. Many of you older people lost husbands, wives, and children to things like diphtheria epidemics or the blizzard of '88. We almost lost the battle against the grasshoppers in the seventies. A lot of farmers and townspeople moved farther west at that time. Then there was the panic of '93. Yes, we've been through a lot in this town's short life. Two years ago we were drawn into another battle. Fights for freedom in two little island countries drew men from our own county. Here's one of them to speak on battles and healing. Our own brother, Frank Sterling."

Frank felt awkward walking up the aisle to the podium before the altar. He was glad he'd badgered Dan into joining him.

He laid his Bible on the podium and opened it, then looked

out over the congregation. He and Dan hadn't told anyone except Bryant that they'd be part of today's service. He saw curiosity in Jason's eyes. Bryant sat beside Andy. Amy and her father sat behind Jason's family, as usual. Frank avoided Amy's gaze. Slim and Shorty sat up front, Slim clutching his cane, both watching Frank in eager expectation.

Frank cleared his throat. "Most of you know my friend, Dan Terrell. We fought together in the Philippines."

Cheers and applause surprised him. He'd grown accustomed to people praising him for fighting but hadn't expected it during the service. When the congregation quieted, he continued.

"Dan's agreed to help me out here. We're not planning to tell you about our war experiences in the Philippines. This Fourth of July, along with celebrating the birth of our country, a lot of people are celebrating the victory in the Spanish-American War. Dan and I would like to suggest we celebrate the peace God has restored. As the reverend indicated, every one of you has had your own wars. You may want to celebrate peace and the end of wars and battles in your own lives.

"Dan and I aren't planning to speak our own words much. We'll be reading from Ecclesiastes three, verses one through eight. Seems to us, this about says it all."

He cleared his throat and began. " 'To every thing there is a season, and a time to every purpose under the heaven.' "

Dan read, " 'A time to be born.' "

Frank purposely roughened his voice in anger. " 'And a time to die.' "

" 'A time to plant.' "

" 'And a time to pluck up that which is planted; A time to kill.' " Frank saw Amy flinch at the words and his tone.

" 'And a time to heal,' " Dan read in a gentle voice.

" 'A time to break down.' "

" 'And a time to build up.' "

" 'A time to weep.' " Frank kept his manner angry.

" 'And a time to laugh.' "

" 'A time to mourn.' "

" 'And a time to dance.' "

" 'A time to cast away stones.' "

" 'And a time to gather stones together. A time to embrace.' "

" 'And a time to refrain from embracing.' "

" 'A time to get.' " Dan's voice seemed to beg Frank to look at the good.

" 'And a time to lose.' " Frank challenged. Then, with a sense of grudging reconsidering, " 'A time to keep.' "

" 'And a time to cast away. A time to rend.' "

" 'And a time to sew.' " Frank's voice was softer now.

" 'A time to keep silence.' "

" 'And a time to speak.' " Frank's voice grew louder, more assured, calmer. " 'A time to love.' "

" 'And a time to hate; A time of war.' "

" 'And a time of peace.' "

The congregation was still as Frank and Dan took their seats. Frank wondered whether the words would mean as much to anyone in the congregation as they meant to him.

After the service, many people stopped to tell him and Dan how much they appreciated their sermon. Amy's thanks meant the most to him. He could see she'd struggled with tears and knew the words had touched her.

He introduced Timothy Bryant to her and saw the sweet modesty reflected in her eyes when Bryant praised her work. Frank was pleased when Amy agreed to allow Bryant to see more of her work before they returned to the farm.

❧

Amy was glad the day was sunny, the light bright through the large windows in the studio at Windom Academy. The light presented her paintings at their best.

She was surprised at the interest Frank's friend showed but kept her curiosity in check. She stood back and allowed Mr.

Bryant to study the paintings at his leisure. He took time to give his full attention to each, one by one: Chalmers sitting on Frank's lap; Pearl on the back porch of the farmhouse staring out at the fields where Jason worked; Slim and Shorty at the depot waving flags at a departing train; Slim in a church pew with a ray of light through a window accenting the wrinkles in his face and the sad longing in his eyes; Viola in a smocked gown squatting in the grass to examine the first violets she'd seen in her young life.

Finally he turned from the paintings. "You have the gift, Miss Henderson."

"Thank you."

"Many artists can paint a portrait that looks like a real person. Only a handful paint portraits of people's hearts and souls. You are one of the few."

Amy blinked back sudden tears. How did he know she'd started seeing that way? How did he know when she painted, she tried to capture the wonder and the pain and the love and the wounds?

She hadn't even known to paint what she saw of a person's heart until she began to understand Frank's wounds. She hadn't known until then that it was possible to see another's heart, let alone paint it.

Mr. Bryant smiled at her. "I know the owners of a fine art gallery in St. Paul. I'm sure they'd love to do a showing of your paintings. May I bring one to them as an example of your work?"

Amy darted a glance of joyful surprise at Frank. He nodded, grinning. "Tim's parents are collectors. You can trust his judgment."

"I–I–I don't know what to say, Mr. Bryant," she stammered.

"A simple yes will suffice."

"Yes." She laughed. "Yes."

"I'd like to buy one of your paintings myself." He pointed

at the canvas of Viola and the flowers. "This one. My wife would love it."

Amy hesitated, loathe to let the painting go.

Mr. Bryant appeared to misunderstand her hesitation. "I'll wait, however, until the showing. That way you will be sure I pay a fair price for it. My friends won't allow your work to be sold for less than its value."

"You seem very sure your friends will like my work as well as you do."

"I am."

Amy allowed herself to share another joy-filled glance with Frank. How wonderful that he had been the one to bring this opportunity into her life. *Thank You, Lord, for allowing him to be here to share this moment with me.*

❧

Behind the curtain that provided privacy for Dr. Matt's patients, Frank struggled only slightly as he slipped his shirt on.

Dr. Matt patted Frank's shoulder. "Your arm's healed well. Must have had a good surgeon in Manila."

"Mm."

"You're fortunate gangrene didn't set in. Battlefield hospitals are filled with patients losing the battle with gangrene. If you'd succumbed to gangrene, you'd likely have lost the rest of your arm, if not your life."

"I know." Frank's response was subdued. Usually he resented the implication that his wound could have been worse, feeling the attitude belittled his loss. Hearing it from Dr. Matt was different. Frank knew the physician had seen worse cases. For that matter, so had Frank. "Saw a few of those cases in the hospital."

"Nothing like a hospital to make a man grateful for what he'd consider a trial otherwise."

"That's saying something." Frank's mind filled with images of patients he'd seen at the hospital. "When I was in the hospital I felt just like you said, grateful. I admit I was worried about getting on with life with only one arm and worried about how people would react. But mostly, I was glad to be alive and glad I wasn't in worse shape."

Dr. Matt lifted graying eyebrows. "Something change?"

"Yes. Me. I let myself get bogged down in self-pity. Let myself?" Frank snorted. "I drove straight into the bog, like I planned it."

"Don't be too hard on yourself. It's a major adjustment for anyone, what you've gone through."

"Well, I'm still alive. I guess that's a pretty good sign God has a plan for the rest of my life. No sense kicking about that."

"Have you been kicking?"

"Like a bronco. Lately, though, I'm beginning to feel like I've got my feet under me again."

Dr. Matt nodded brusquely. "You'll make it. Some men don't when life gets tough, but you will. I've seen you make it through other hard places. Let's head out to the apothecary, and I'll get you those pain powders."

When he left the apothecary, Frank climbed the stairs to the Hendersons' apartment. He'd received a letter from Bryant the day before. Enclosed with it was a letter for Amy. Bryant had asked him to deliver it.

It took more courage than Frank liked to admit to climb those stairs. He'd barely spoken to Amy's father since returning to Chippewa City. Whenever they saw each other at church, Mr. Henderson was cordial, but he never smiled. Frank couldn't blame him. He stood before the door to the apartment, took a deep breath to steady his courage, and knocked. He slid his hat from his head before the door opened.

"Frank. This is a surprise."

*Not a happy one,* Frank surmised from the older man's scowl. "Hello, Sir. I've brought some mail for Amy."

"She isn't home." Mr. Henderson stepped back. "Won't you come in?"

Frank entered reluctantly. He set his hat on the table beside the door so he could pull the letter from his pocket. "Here you are, Sir."

Mr. Henderson held the envelope at arm's length and peered at it. Then he appeared to remember the wire-rimmed glasses he held in his other hand. He put them on and looked at the packet again. "Oh, yes. From your friend Mr. Bryant."

"I'll just be going, Sir." Frank reached for his hat.

"No, please, stay for a few minutes."

Frank hesitated.

"It was a nice thing you did for her, showing that man her paintings." The words were said in a grudging tone.

"She's a talented artist."

"Yes. Amy tells me I'm not to be angry with you for breaking your engagement."

Frank stared at him, surprised to silence.

"She says you have every right to change your mind about marrying her, and she wouldn't want you if you don't want her." Mr. Henderson shook his head. "Have to tell you, Son, I'm not so forgiving of your treatment of my daughter as she is."

"I don't know that I deserve forgiveness, Sir. I do know Amy deserves a better man than me."

"You're not expecting an argument on that point, I hope."

"No, Sir." Frank made himself stand still and face Mr. Henderson's accusing gaze.

Finally the older man nodded, as though he'd made a decision. "There's something I'd like you to see. Come over to my desk."

Frank followed him across the room to the corner where the elegant mahogany desk from the Hendersons' more prosperous days stood near the window. Clipped newspaper articles and books covered the top of the desk.

On one corner stood the music box Frank had given Amy for Christmas years ago. On top of the walnut base a man and woman skated within a crystal snow globe. His heart caught at the sight. He'd bought the music box for Amy because ice-skating held special memories for them. Would life ever again seem as innocent and beautiful as it had the first time they'd skated together at the millpond?

Mr. Henderson nodded toward the piles on the desk. "This is Amy's project. Go ahead and look."

Frank stepped backward, shocked at the idea of invading Amy's privacy. "I don't think so, Sir."

"Nothing personal here." Mr. Henderson held up a newspaper clipping. "No secrets; just news about the war."

"The war?" Almost against his will, Frank read the headline of the article Amy's father held toward him.

"Amy reads everything she can find about the war, on all fronts. She pours over soldiers' personal experiences and pictures published in the papers."

"Sounds gruesome."

"Yes, I thought so. Hardly a proper topic for feminine pursuit."

Frank agreed with the sentiment. He couldn't imagine sweet-hearted, refined Amy thrilling to war stories. "I thought she hated war."

"She does. But she loves you." Mr. Henderson shook his head. "I don't know why, but she does."

Frank's neck and face grew warm from shame.

Mr. Henderson shuffled some of the papers and lifted a book he found beneath them.

Frank recognized it: Teddy Roosevelt's tales of the Rough Riders in Cuba. He'd heard others speak of it. Experiencing war firsthand had left him with no desire to read of others' battles.

"My daughter fills her mind with all of this for only one reason."

Frank met Mr. Henderson's gaze. "And that is?"

"To understand you better. She doesn't want to remain oblivious to the things you've seen."

"I wouldn't want her to see what I've seen!"

The tense lines in Amy's father's face softened, and so did his voice. "Of course you wouldn't. No gentleman would want any woman to know the horrors of war."

"Especially not Amy."

"I've told her it's not necessary. She insists it is."

Frank stared down at the cluttered desk. Consternation drained away into wonder that Amy loved him enough to do this for him. Even though he'd pushed her away, tried to keep her from his life, she'd struggled to understand him, his pain, his world. She'd struggled to give love to him when he wasn't aware of her efforts. Her choice reminded him of Christ's choice to become part of humanity and experience man's struggles.

Love enwrapped him in such a tangible manner, it felt almost like being held in Amy's embrace.

Mr. Henderson held out the letter from Timothy Bryant. "Maybe you should deliver this to Amy yourself. She's at Windom Academy, painting."

❧

"Funny thing about watches."

Amy whirled around at the sound of Frank's voice. Blue paint dripped from the tip of the brush she held in her right hand. Frank sat on a stool near the door of the studio. "How long have you been here? I didn't hear you come in."

He grinned and nodded toward the canvas behind her. "You were a bit engrossed in that painting. As I was saying," he held the watch she'd given him before he left for the war, "it's a funny thing about watches."

A little thrill ran through her that he still carried the watch.

He started winding the watch. She could hear the soft action of metal against metal. "Watches stop keeping time if we don't remember to wind them," he continued.

She wanted to giggle at his philosophical tone. "I've noticed that."

He looked up from the watch, smiling. "It took me awhile to learn how to wind this with one hand."

Her heart skipped a beat at the simple fact. Even the watch she'd given him to remind him of her love had become something that reminded him of his wound. But. . .his eyes didn't hold the look of pain today. She wasn't sure what was happening, but if he was willing to spend a few happy minutes with her, she wasn't about to protest.

"Sorry. I got sidetracked. What was I saying?"

He didn't look like he'd forgotten. He looked like he was teasing her.

"You were saying what a funny thing it is that watches need to be wound."

"Mm. Yes. I mean, watches are supposed to keep time. But time can't be kept, can it?" His voice softened. His gaze met hers, unwavering. "It can't be kept, and it can't be stopped."

"No," she whispered, suddenly feeling breathless.

"I told you once that I'd love you even if time stopped."

"I remember."

"Time doesn't stop. Neither has my love."

Amy caught her breath, hardly able to believe what she was hearing. "Frank—"

" 'To every thing there is a season,' Amy, 'and a time to every purpose under heaven.' Since you gave me this watch, I've been through times of war, times of mourning, times of casting away, times of healing. Lots of times. For awhile I forgot time doesn't stop, and after war comes peace, and after mourning comes dancing. I tried to forget there's a time for embracing and a time for loving. I was afraid those times were behind me and would never come again."

Amy trembled. She longed to go to him, but he'd distanced

himself from her for so long that she hadn't the courage to without his express invitation.

He stood and slipped the watch into his trouser pocket. He crossed the room slowly, his gaze never leaving hers. When he reached her, he removed the palette from her left hand and set it down on a nearby table. Then he took the brush from her and laid that down.

He faced her from about a foot away. "Ecclesiastes tells us there's a time to keep silence and a time to speak. I've kept silent a long time. Tim Bryant says you see into hearts, so I guess it won't do me any good to keep pretending I'm strong and tough where I'm not. I'd like to believe I'm ready for a time of love again."

Confusion dampened her joy. Why, if he loved her, did he keep this distance between them?

Her confusion must have shown, for he held up his hand as though in warning. "I haven't treated you well for the last year. I don't know if my time of being ready to love again coincides with your time of being ready to love again. Maybe you need a time of healing, a time of healing from the wounds I've inflicted on you. If so, I understand."

Now she saw the pain in his brown eyes clearly and the hope behind the pain. Her own hope leaped to life in response. "You haven't done anything unforgivable. Besides, isn't it love that heals wounds?"

The tension in his face melted away into a smile. "When I left for the war, I asked you to meet me with a promise. . .the promise that you'd still marry me."

"I remember."

"I'm a bit late claiming that promise. Or perhaps claiming is too strong a word."

Joy burst from her heart. "My promise still holds."

Finally he took the step that bridged the distance between them. Amy closed her eyes and sighed in deep contentment as he pulled her close in his embrace.

For many minutes they stood like that, glorying in the gift of being together. It felt so familiar: the way his head rested against hers, the way his shoulders felt beneath her hands, the sound of his heartbeat beneath her cheek. It was the place that felt most right to her of all places on earth.

"I hate that I haven't two arms to hold you, Amy." His whisper was rough with anguish. "I can't help it. No matter how much I try not to mind, I do."

"I know, my love." Tears misted her eyes. She blinked them back. She ached to make his pain go away, but she'd learned over the last year that it wasn't in her power to do that. "But what's most important is that your heart holds me."

"Even if time stops." His lips touched her temple, kissed the edge of her eyebrow with the lightness of a feather, moved at long last to meet her lips. His kiss was warm and sweet and lingering.

He pulled away only far enough to whisper against her lips, "I love you, Amy. I'll always love you."

For so long she'd wondered whether she'd ever hear those words again. They were sweeter to her than any other words could possibly be.

For a long while they were lost in each other's embraces and kisses, speaking their love for each other, rejoicing that they'd found each other once more, shyly revealing how much they'd missed each other during the last two years.

More than an hour passed before Frank asked, "Will you marry me after harvest is over?"

Amy smiled mischievously. "Do we need to wait that long?"

He caught her close again with a laugh. "If you come out to the farm as my wife before then, you won't have time to finish the paintings for your show."

"What show?"

He released her then and pulled an envelope from his pocket.

"This came today from Tim Bryant."

She opened it eagerly and scanned its contents. "You're right, Frank. His friends want to do a showing of my work in November." She could hardly believe so much happiness was coming to her at one time. A thought stopped her. She looked up at Frank. "Will you mind if my work is shown? I probably won't have much time to paint after we're married."

"Between being a farmer's wife and raising our children, you mean?" His eyes twinkled.

She felt herself blush at his reference to children. She leaned against him, smiling. "Yes."

"We'll find a way for you to paint. Like Tim said, you have a gift for it. Besides, I want paintings of all of our children."

Amy laughed, lifting her eyebrows in teasing query. "All of them? How many are you planning?"

"As many as the good Lord grants."

Amy relaxed into his kiss, thanking God that at last they had returned to the time to love.

# A Letter To Our Readers

Dear Reader:

In order that we might better contribute to your reading enjoyment, we would appreciate your taking a few minutes to respond to the following questions. We welcome your comments and read each form and letter we receive. When completed, please return to the following:

Rebecca Germany, Fiction Editor
Heartsong Presents
PO Box 719
Uhrichsville, Ohio 44683

1. Did you enjoy reading *Meet Me with a Promise* by JoAnn A. Grote?

❑ Very much! I would like to see more books by this author!

❑ Moderately. I would have enjoyed it more if

_______________________________________________

_______________________________________________

2. Are you a member of **Heartsong Presents**? Yes ❑ No ❑
If no, where did you purchase this book?______________

_______________________________________________

3. How would you rate, on a scale from 1 (poor) to 5 (superior), the cover design?_________________________

4. On a scale from 1 (poor) to 10 (superior), please rate the following elements.

| | |
|---|---|
| _____ Heroine | _____ Plot |
| _____ Hero | _____ Inspirational theme |
| _____ Setting | _____ Secondary characters |

5. These characters were special because________________

______________________________________________

______________________________________________

6. How has this book inspired your life?_______________

______________________________________________

______________________________________________

7. What settings would you like to see covered in future **Heartsong Presents** books?________________________

______________________________________________

______________________________________________

8. What are some inspirational themes you would like to see treated in future books?________________________

______________________________________________

______________________________________________

9. Would you be interested in reading other **Heartsong Presents** titles? Yes ❑ No ❑

10. Please check your age range:

❑ Under 18 ❑ 18-24 ❑ 25-34

❑ 35-45 ❑ 46-55 ❑ Over 55

Name ____________________________________

Occupation ______________________________

Address _________________________________

City _______________ State __________ Zip __________

Email ___________________________________